"Facts are facts," Jenny's mother said. "Everybody needs a burial plot sooner or later. Everyone passes away. My parents, God rest them, passed away. When people get to be senior citizens, their time is coming closer every day, and there's no use pretending it isn't so. . . ."

NORMA FOX MAZER is the author of many well-known books for young adults, including *Someone to Love*; *Up in Seth's Room*; *Dear Bill, Remember Me?*; *Saturday, the Twelfth of October*; and *Summer Girls, Love Boys*, all available in Dell Laurel-Leaf editions, and *I, Trissy*, available in a Dell Yearling edition. She lives in Jamesville, New York.

# A Figure of Speech

## Norma Fox Mazer

LAUREL-LEAF BOOKS bring together under a single imprint
outstanding works of fiction and nonfiction particularly suit-
able for young adult readers, both in and out of the classroom.
Charles F. Reasoner, Professor Emeritus of Children's Liter-
ature and Reading, New York University, is consultant to this
series.

Published by
Dell Publishing
a division of
The Bantam Doubleday Dell Publishing Group, Inc.
666 Fifth Avenue
New York, New York 10103

ISBN: 0-440-94374-4

RL: 4.9

Reprinted by arrangement with Delacorte Press

Printed in the United States of America

One Previous Dell Edition

April 1989

10

RAD

*For H. I. M.*

# Chapter 1

In a restaurant Jenny is serving coffee and sticky rolls to the people. Her mother calls her. "This coffee is cold and the rolls are stale!"

Jenny hurries to take the offending foods away. Her mother is sitting with important people. "Can I have a peach?" Jenny says.

"Do you deserve it?" her mother demands.

Grandpa puts his arm around Jenny. "Grandpa will fix things," he says, but when she looks up, she feels extremely worried. Is it really Grandpa? He's wearing white pants, a white jacket, and has Band Aids plastered to his forehead in the shape of a cross.

Jenny feels afraid. "Take that off!" she says. "Click! Click!" Or is it "Quick! Quick!"? . . .

Jenny sat up in bed, the fragments of her dream slipping along the edges of her mind. Her stomach was still chugging fearfully, and there was an aftertaste in her throat, a sourness she swallowed as she looked around the dim bedroom she shared with her sisters. They were both still sound asleep, the baby's behind humped up like a turtle, Gail with the blankets pulled over her head, her bare feet sticking out below.

It was Thursday morning. The window next to Jenny's bed was beaded with rain. The electric clock on the bureau said six-ten. In the street a car backfired like a gunshot. No one else in the house was awake or stirring. No, that wasn't quite right. Listening, she heard Grandpa moving below in the basement apartment. She wanted to call him. Grandpa! Hello, Grandpa! The last of the dream sadness left her. She pushed aside the covers and, restraining her impulse to jump out of bed, cautiously and quietly put her bare feet down on the cold linoleum-covered floor.

She pulled on jeans, then eased open a bureau drawer. It creaked and she stopped, motionless, holding her breath. The thing was to get dressed without waking Gail, then to get through the house without waking her mother and go downstairs for an early morning visit with Grandpa. She edged the drawer open farther and pulled out the first sweater her hand touched. Ugh! A grassy green one passed on from Gail. She slipped it over her head, picked up her sneakers, and tiptoed across the room, avoiding the spot that creaked.

The baby had kicked off her blankets and Jenny pulled them back over her. Ethel's lashes fluttered. Shhh, baby. Jenny crept past her. In her sleep, Gail sighed. Jenny froze. If Gail woke, that was it. She'd have to go back to bed. "Don't!" Gail said, and flopped over, pulling the blankets with her.

Jenny turned the knob of the door, stepped out into the hall, and tiptoed to the bathroom. Could water be run softly? Jenny tried, catching a few silent drops to wash her hands and face. She brushed her teeth, staring at herself in the mirror. Modigliani girl. That was what Mrs. Spencer who taught math in Alliance Junior High had called her. All the girls liked to babysit for the Spencers, even though the two kids were sort of spoiled (Chris had bitten Jenny once), because the Spencers had a way of making you feel important. Besides, they always overpaid.

"Jenny, did you ever see any paintings by the Italian painter Modigliani?" Mrs. Spencer had asked several weeks ago. Jenny shook her head and snatched a crayon Kim was about to stuff into her mouth. "You could have been one of his models," Mrs. Spencer said. "All eyes and that narrow, delicate chin."

For days Jenny had walked around in a cloud of vanity. Modigliani girl! A painter's model! Last Saturday she and Rhoda Rivers had taken the bus downtown, run up the wide gray steps of the public library, had entered the cool silence of the Music and Art Room, and without too much trouble had found a large glossy book of modern art. They had thumbed through the pictures. Disappointment! The Modigliani faces were crooked, the eyes lopsided, and as Rhoda said, all the girls old Modig painted looked as if they had a bad case of toothache.

Picking up her sneakers again, Jenny turned the bathroom doorknob stealthily, put her feet down like a cat, and came face to face with her mother.

"I thought I heard the water running," Mrs. Pennoyer said. Holding her red chenille robe around herself, Mrs. Pennoyer stood squarely in Jenny's way. "What do you think you're doing, anyway? Why are you up so early?"

"I woke up, so I got up. I was quiet," Jenny said.

"Shhh! You'll wake everyone. Go back to bed and sleep some more."

"I'm not sleepy, Mom."

"Go on back, anyway. It's too early to get up."

"Grandpa gets up early. I was going to visit him."

"For heaven's sake, this is carrying things too far. Six o'clock in the morning! This is ridiculous," her mother whispered. "Don't you spend enough time with your grandfather?"

"Mom—"

"Every extra minute with him, whenever I look for you, you're downstairs. Your father's noticed the same thing. What do you do down there?"

"We talk, and play cards, and—" Jenny waved her hands helplessly. She didn't have to *do* anything, only *be* with Grandpa.

"You ought to like being with your family a little more," her mother said.

"Grandpa *is* my family."

"You know what I mean. Don't act thick on purpose. Why are you standing here, arguing with me at this time of morning?" Mrs. Pennoyer gave Jenny a little push. "Back to bed till it's time to get up. Go on, now."

Cheeks stinging, Jenny did as she was told. She got into bed fully dressed and lay with her hands under her head, biting her lips, twitching, and turning. At a quarter to seven, Ethel staggered up from under her covers, grabbed her crib bars, and began shaking them. Then Jenny heard her father go into the bathroom, clearing his throat loudly. Gail's head, covered with rows of pink foam curlers, emerged from the mound of blankets. "What time is it?" she said thickly, peering at the clock. She sat up and began taking the rollers out of her hair. Jenny pushed aside the blankets for the second time that morning, and Gail looked at her in astonishment. "What'd you do, sleep in your clothes, idiot child?"

"Forget it," Jenny said. She peeled off the grassy green sweater. She wasn't going to wear that rag to school.

# *Chapter 2*

Jenny's grandfather, Carl Pennoyer, woke at his usual hour, groaning with his aches. Stiff in the shoulders, stiff in the back, stiff and aching everywhere. "Oh, Mother, Mother," he muttered, groaning as he sat up in the iron bed and threw aside the covers with swollen fingers.

The air in the room was damp and smelled sooty. The old man always slept with the window opened wide, letting in the damp cool night air, despite the fact that it wasn't always the best thing for him, not with his aches and pains, his stiff swollen joints, and aching legs and fingers.

He reached toward his toes and moaned again, flexing his fingers and forcing himself to reach and stretch. He slept in his underwear, baggy shorts and a limp undershirt with thin shoulder straps. "Oh, Mother, Mother," he moaned again, dropping his bare feet to the floor. He was a long, bony old man with long, bony yellow toes and nails that grew as thick as horn.

He pushed down the window. It was six o'clock and it was raining outside. Why did he wake at such an hour every morning? Six o'clock. He had nothing to get up for at six o'clock every morning. No work to go to. No cows to milk, no factory card to punch on the dot of the hour. He could sleep until eight o'clock, ten o'clock, until noon, and no one would care. Nothing would change. The world's work got done without him, he thought, beginning to feel sorry for himself. Then his eyes fell on a clear plastic book bag that Jenny had left downstairs the day before. She was always forgetting things in his apartment—school books, papers, a comb, a pair of gloves, once even her shoes. Carl picked up the book bag from the floor and put it carefully on his bureau. The pang of self-pity faded. Of course he had a reason to get out of bed every morning. Jenny. She was his reason.

He yawned and scratched the sparse gray hairs on his chest. Flexing his fingers, he walked around in his bare feet, walking out the aches and stiffness in his joints. It was chilly in the apartment, the windows shone wetly, and beads of moisture hung on the walls. The old man's apartment was part of the cellar of his son's home, and the outer walls often sweated.

He put on a shabby brown sweater with buttons down the front and two sagging pockets, and went into the little closet with a toilet. He stood in front of the bowl for a long time. Everything was more difficult when you were eighty-three years old. It was strange to be old, he thought, to have lived eighty-three years, to have knobby hands with arthritis bunching up the knuckles, and breath that didn't always go smoothly in and out of his body. It was strange to be so old and remember so many things and think that so much was gone.

In his kitchen—no more than a wall with open shelves for dishes and pots, a sink, a two-burner stove, and a tiny refrigerator—he washed with cold water, gasping and shaking his head like a dog as the water ran down his neck. He could have washed with warm water, but he had begun his life washing with cold water, had continued washing with cold water in his prime, and now in his old age it was a matter of honor.

He finished dressing. His pants sagged on his waistline, sagged on his flat buttocks. He tightened his belt. He had never been fat, but there had been years of his life when firm smooth flesh covered his bones, when he was proud of his muscles and his strength and looked for ways to impress his wife. Good-looking fellow, that Carl Pennoyer—that was the opinion of those who knew him, and his own opinion as well. Good-looking, smart, strong, and plenty capable.

The tea kettle was whistling. He poured hot water into a cup and dipped in a tea bag. He took two aspirins from a bottle on the shelf and chewed them, then stood at the window that looked out onto street level. He gulped his burning tea, scalding his throat. He always drank everything too hot: soup, tea, coffee; he had gulped the burning liquid greedily when he was young, and now that he was old he did it from force of habit. This had always irritated Frances, his wife. "You'll burn your throat," she warned irritably, and always added, "Carl, stop that gulping!" To annoy her, he'd gulp as quickly as ever and with good loud sound effects. To get back at him, she gave him lukewarm coffee, soup tepid as a bath, and tea so cool he could have washed his face in it.

Carl allowed himself a smile. He had lived an ordinary life and parts of it were completely lost to him (he couldn't, for instance, remember what his father had looked like), but other things—sometimes the oldest things—he remembered perfectly: on a dark cold night huddled against his mother in a train . . . plush seats, smell of cinders, grinding sleepy rhythm of the train, and the warmth of his mother's leg through her dress. "Carl, you'll mess me up." But she had let him go on leaning heavily, drowsily, next to her. They were on their way upstate to his grandparents' farm where they went every summer. The farm—for little Carl, it was a golden place of light and shining space . . . field after field of grass and grain . . . the milking cows, the goats, and the turkeys in the trees. He had been allowed to roam at will, to climb trees, to lie buried in the grass with bugs tickling his legs and the sun burning his ears. . . . He remembered the fresh white juice of an apple running down his chin, whipped cream pies, the cream thick as snow, and his grandfather handing him a dipper with warm foaming milk he'd just taken from the cow. "Here, boy, drink up. Nothing like this in the city."

Outside, the rain dripped. Cars were already packed bumper to bumper on Pittmann Street, fumes clouding the air, headlights blurry in the gloom, windshield wipers ticking monotonously. The old man unwrapped a piece of stale bread and poured another cup of boiling tea. He no longer ate much—two cups of boiling tea and a piece of stale bread was his usual breakfast. He dipped the bread into the tea and sucked on it. Bread today was a disappointment compared to the thick, dark, almost bitter black bread of his childhood. For a moment he almost had the taste of that bread on his tongue. He remembered foods he'd eaten, and he remembered making love, and walking for miles on a blazing day with sweat dripping into his eyes, and he remembered burying three children before his son Frank was born.

Upstairs, over his head, he heard the first vigorous stirrings of his son's family. Muffled voices, thumps, yells, feet rushing this way and that, doors opening and then slamming shut. The house upstairs seemed to vibrate with life: *thump! smash! crack!* The baby cried, someone yelled, someone else laughed. But downstairs, down here in his half dark apartment, down here half in the earth, he disturbed no one, made no hustle or bustle or loud noises as he drank his tea and looked at the wet, shiny sidewalk and the occasional pair of feet that flapped by his window.

After a while he glanced at the clock. Startled, he realized he had been dreaming. Time had passed, and Jenny would soon be down for her morning visit. He mustn't let her catch him sitting around woolgathering like an old man. He brought his teacup into the kitchen and rinsed it under the hot water tap. The hot water felt good, and he rinsed his cup carefully, letting the hot water warm his hands.

At the sound of the expected knock, he dried his hands and pulled a yellow newspaper from one of the stacks of newspapers piled against the wall, and sat down at the metal table beneath the window. "All right, come in," he said in his usual voice, grumpy and harsh as the cry of an old crow. "Come in whoever it is."

Jenny entered. "Good morning, Grandpa! It's me, of course." She was wearing plaid slacks and a blue raincoat. A speck of toothpaste was caught on her upper lip. The old man pretended to see none of it.

"You're late this morning," he said crossly.

"Am I? Really? I was up lots earlier. I wanted to come down, but Mom wouldn't let me." She leaned over his shoulder to look at the yellowed newspaper. "What year are you reading today? My year! I was born that year."

"And Frances, your grandmother, died that year."

Jenny put her cheek against his. "It makes you sad to think about Grandmother. Don't be sad, Grandpa."

Carl felt dazzled. He could have sat that way forever, with the fresh cool cheek of his granddaughter pressed against his face.

"I was sad this morning," she said. "When I first woke up. I had the weirdest dream, about you and me and Mom. It was so crazy. When I woke up, I felt just like crying, as if you were going away from me."

He wet his thumb and turned over a page of the newspaper. "I ain't going any place," he said. "I've been here all your life, haven't I?"

The same month that his wife had died, Jenny had been born. Jenny, unplanned and in the way. His daughter-in-law, Amelia, had three other little babies to look after—Vince, Frankie, and Gail. Vince, the oldest, had been only six, so Amelia had her hands full, and then along came the infant Jenny to bother her even more.

At the same time the old man had moved out of

the home he and Frances had shared, and into the basement apartment of his son's house. Everything was so strange, so strange and queer without Frances; sometimes the feeling came over him that a good wind could blow him away. And then living in a cellar, being alone so much, and when not alone, getting into busy people's ways. Jenny was in the way, too, so he put her in her carriage one day and wheeled her around. Amelia had been grateful. After that he wheeled her every day all over the neighborhood—Pittmann Street, Jericho Hill, Catherine Avenue, Brewer Road—everywhere. When she outgrew the carriage, and then the stroller, he held her hand and they walked together. They became inseparable companions; he had never been that close to a child before—not to his living son, Frank, who was Jenny's father, not to any of his other grandchildren. He had never pushed a carriage or a stroller, or willingly walked for hours with a child's hot, moist hand in his own. Not till Jenny. His darling, his precious, his light.

"Well, what are you waiting for?" he said to her. "You'll be late for school." He yanked the paper away from her. "Go on, get going."

She pulled on a pointed shiny blue rain hat and tied the strings under her chin. "See you later, Grandpa. Save that newspaper for me to read, okay? How funny and old-fashioned things were in the olden days." She ran out, slamming the door.

Carl smoothed the yellowed newspaper in front of him. The olden days! The newspaper was only thirteen years old. Thirteen years—they had passed in a moment. He would have liked to have newspapers that were fifty years old, or sixty years old, or eighty years old. And still that wouldn't have been the olden days, not to him. But since he didn't have such papers, the ones he'd begun collecting after Frances died would have to do. He found it soothing, satisfying, to read about the disasters and tragedies of years ago.

Terrible things had happened—wars, floods, hurricanes, drunken drivers, and maddened men with guns. Oh, the papers were daily full of such awful events, and yet the world was still here, and so was he. Yes, so was he.

# Chapter 3

Jenny was walking behind Gail down Pittmann Street. It was still raining, a spongy, relentless September rain that pressed the fumes and garbagy odors of the city close to the ground. Jenny had lived on Pittmann Street all her life. She knew without looking that in the window of Richter's Open-All-Night Groceteria faded cardboard Coke signs nudged plastic flowers and a dusty tower of canned soups. She knew that the Baldwins (who live in the leaning pink frame house with a catalpa tree in the bare front yard) had three cars; and the Rimbauds (who lived in a green frame house with clotheslines strung on the porch) were mourning the recent death in a traffic accident of their retarded son, Nicky. She had watched the Pittmann Arms, a multi-dwelling apartment building, rise from a churned-up mudhole in the ground to its present raw splendor. And she could name every dog, every cat, and every kid between the ages of eight and eighteen in every house and apartment up and down the street.

"Jenny!" Gail called, looking back. "Are you coming? Don't poke along so!" Carrying a clear bubble umbrella over her head, Gail sidestepped a puddle.

"Don't wait for me," Jenny yelled. She had to yell to be heard over the sound of traffic. Cars, bumper to bumper, poured through Pittmann Street in a frenzied rush toward the carpet mill, the iron works, and the pharmaceutical factory. "Go on!" she yelled. "Go

ahead. Go, go!" With her long legs, she could easily
have overtaken Gail. What for? So they could argue?
There was exactly one year and a million miles of
difference between them. Jenny was stork thin; Gail
cat plump. Jenny was dark haired, dark eyed, impatient, and energetic. Gail, with sandy hair and light
blue eyes, was slow and bossy. Being older, she took
it to be her duty to note if Jenny brushed her teeth,
changed her underwear, did her homework, and went
to bed on time. This was intolerable to Jenny; in the
past she'd often gone for Gail, flailing, pummeling,
and screeching out her resentment and anger.

Once, about a year before, Gail had taken a piece
of yellow chalk and drawn a thick line around Jenny's
bed and bureau. "There, brat. Don't you cross that
line without my permission."

"Am I supposed to fly when I want to leave the
room?" Jenny began flapping her wings and cackling
like a crazy bird.

"Shut up!" Gail said.

"Make me! Make me!" Jenny flapped her wings
faster and faster, cackling and jumping around Gail.

"Stop that!"

"Stop what? What? What?" Jenny cackled.

"Mother. Mo-ther!" Gail screamed.

"Jenny, you stop that wildness," her mother called.

But Jenny couldn't stop. Carried away by her im-
personation of a large crazy bird, she kept whirling
and flapping, jumping and cackling until her mother
marched in and slapped her.

"I didn't even start it. She did," Jenny said, her
hand on her stinging cheek. "You're unfair!"

"I don't want to hear any more. You have a big
mouth, and you'll get another slap if you're not careful."

Later Jenny had taken a sheet of lined school paper,
divided it in half, and made two headings:

ASSETS:
1. Grandpa
2. Strong legs

LIABILITIES:
1. Big mouth
2. Middle girl
3. Not liked as much by parents as Gail and Ethel
4. Being ignored by Frankie and Vince
5. Too skinny
6. Funny looks
   a. big nose
   b. big mouth
   c. nothing-special eyes

It had seemed to be a very short list of assets and a very long list of liabilities. But after she showed it to Grandpa, he had said, "You left something out of that first section. Out of Assets—a questioning mind."

She had written that in immediately. "3. Questioning mind." Then she asked Grandpa, since he considered a questioning mind so fine, would he answer any questions she asked.

"I don't know what you've got going on in that head," he said. "Sounds like a trap to me. I'll answer as many questions as I can. There are some things I don't know."

"Well, of course," she said. "I never thought you knew everything."

"Didn't you, though?" Grandpa had said, looking miffed.

Ahead of Jenny, Gail disappeared around the corner. Jenny leaped over a puddle. She didn't mind the rain in her face; in fact, she liked it. She ran up Jericho Hill, and at the corner of Hazard Street, Rhoda was waiting. "Jenny Pennoyer!" Rhoda cried.

"Rhoda Rivers!"

"I'll be goldanged!"

"Can say that again!"

As if they didn't meet nearly every morning to walk to school, exchanging news, gossip, teasing, and jokes.

"New elephant joke," Rhoda said. "How can you tell if an elephant's been in the refrigerator?"

Jenny groaned. "I bite. How?"

"Naturally, by the footprints in the margarine. What's the difference between an elephant and a raccoon wearing purple sunglasses?"

"You know I hate these jokes."

"The elephant's wearing blue sunglasses."

"That's so stupid," Jenny screamed, laughing.

Rhoda smirked. She was a short, eager girl with a full head of frizzy hair. "Where do baby elephants come from?"

"I refuse to answer."

"BIG storks." She linked arms with Jenny. "So—what's new, what's fresh, what's outrageous this morning?"

"My father was ranting at Frankie again last night. Called him a 'crazy mole.' Said he runs around like a crazy mole too much."

"Doesn't your father know that boy might be an Olympic runner some day?"

Jenny shook her head. "Not Frankie. He just likes to run."

*If he ran in a race,* Jenny's father had said, *if he tried to win medals, or if he was on the cross-country team, I'd understand.* But Frankie ran alone.

"He doesn't care about winning or anything like that," Jenny said. "Just running."

"I could like that boy a whole lot," Rhoda said. "How come he doesn't know I'm living and breathing and ready to be passionately in love with him?"

"I'll give him the message."

"Don't you dare!"

"Don't you want to build up his ego?"

"No!"

Jenny wouldn't let it go. "Where's your public spirit? Your compassion? Your heart? Listen, I'll tell

Frankie, 'Rhoda Rivers has a mad, passionate, secret thing for you—' "

"Forget it! Forget I said anything!"

" 'She wants to whisper elephant jokes in your ear.' "

"Jenny! You fink."

"And his eyes will open wide—"

"Those sleepy eyes. Fat chance," Rhoda said, giggling.

"And this big grin will come to his face, and he'll be so set up he won't care what my father says to him."

"Does he care now?"

"I'll say. When my father goes after him about running or not doing good in school, you should see Frankie's face."

One day in a bookstore called The Paper Place, Jenny had seen a book called *The Loneliness of the Long Distance Runner*. Frankie! she thought, and she bought the book. As it turned out it was short stories, only the first one being about a runner; and the runner, although a boy, wasn't much like Frankie at all, since he was English and a thief and had been sent to reform school. But there was a line in the story that caught Jenny's imagination at once: "It's a treat being a long distance runner, out in the world by yourself, with not a soul to make you bad tempered or tell you what to do." She read that several times, wondering if that was why Frankie ran. Frankie, her sleepy-eyed, mop-headed, sullen, strange, running brother. She'd never quite understood him until then; and even so, she wasn't sure that she really did. But maybe she was closer.

She wanted to give the book to her father, but didn't quite dare. What if he took it the wrong way? Thought she meant that Frankie would grow up to be a thief and get sent to reform school? She gave the book to Frankie, anyway, but as far as she knew he'd

never even cracked the first page. Disappointing. But
that was the way things seemed to work out a lot.
People misunderstood each other, fought, disagreed,
couldn't get together, never said what they really
meant. People who ought to have been close—her
father and Frankie, she and Gail, she and her mother.
Oh, yes! She and her mother.

Her father could be sharp with her, often was, but
between Jenny and her mother there ran a deep,
underlying irritation. Jenny had first become con-
scious of it when she was eleven, and had gone
through phases trying to break that secret rawness.
She had, quite easily, gone through a terrifically bratty
phase, doing a lot of kicking and screaming, which
only got her confined to her room day after day. Then
she tried being "sweet and good," but the strain of it
all was too much, and after a week or so she reverted
to normal. Another time, after reading *Little Women*,
she prayed diligently for her mother to be transformed
into a Marmie-Mother, gentle, understanding . . . and
perfect, while visions of herself as sweet as Beth and
smart as Jo danced in her head. In the end it all came
down to the same thing—she was Jenny, her mother
was her mother, and nothing changed.

Rhoda tugged at her arm. "You're daydreaming.
Want to sleep over Friday night?"

"I'll ask."

"When's your brother Vince coming for a visit?"
Rhoda, being an only child, found Jenny's family of
brothers and sisters enviable.

"He just went back to college a couple of weeks ago,
but Thanksgiving, I guess," Jenny said. "If he doesn't
go to some girl's house like he did last year." Ever
since he'd been fifteen, girls had been calling Vince
on the phone and ringing the Pennoyer doorbell to
say, "Is Vince in? I was just passing in the neighborhood and thought I'd ask." In his senior year at Alliance High, Vince had been voted "Best Personality

and Handsomest Boy." Now that he was away at college, Jenny was sure that girls were still crazy about him. She would be, too, if she was older and not his sister. He had fantastic eyes, like Omar Sharif, and had grown a mustache that her father hated, but that she adored.

"Listen," Rhoda said, "let me know when Lover Boy comes home. I want to come over and drool a little."

# Chapter 4

That night at suppertime the Pennoyer family was all gathered around the table. Jenny had come flying in last and received her father's disapproving stare. He believed in promptness and was always ready to sit down at the dining room table at exactly five forty-five. "Grace, Jenny," he ordered.

Jenny folded her hands and looked down. "Bless this supper, oh Lord, and thank You for providing for the Pennoyer family. Amen. I'm starved. Pass the hamburgers, Gail."

"Say, please."

"Pass the hamburgers!"

"Mom gets them first," Gail said virtuously, passing the wide blue dish to Mrs. Pennoyer.

"What happened in school today, Frankie?" Mr. Pennoyer, napkin tucked firmly into his shirt collar, reached for the salad bowl.

Frankie shook his head. "Same as usual. Nothing."

"What do you mean—nothing?"

Frankie stuffed bread in his mouth. "Just nothing."

"How could nothing happen? You were in school all day, weren't you? Now what happened in school today?"

Frankie twisted in his seat, then slumped down on his spine. "Uh—nothing. I can't think of anything."

"You went to classes. You were there. Tell me something that went on, something you learned."

Frankie's eyes were squeezed nearly shut. Jenny threw her brother a sympathetic glance. She hated these inquisitions. Questions and answers, just like school. "We had assembly today," she said, trying to kick Frankie under the table. "Mr. Bastable from the City Environmental Agency talked to us about the Citizens Clean Up Your City Program. CCUYCP. Remember, Frankie?"

"Were you at the assembly or not?" Mr. Pennoyer said. Frankie nodded. "Well, what did you get out of it?"

"Get out of it?" Frankie repeated. His face was twisted as if he were in dreadful pain. "Get out of it," he said again. He shook his head. "Well—not much, I guess."

"Seems like you don't get much out of anything," Mr. Pennoyer said. "That's because you don't put enough *into* anything to get much *out* of it. Do you think I'd be assistant manager for a large supermarket if I didn't put anything into my job? I started as a stock boy and I went up to become assistant manager."

Everyone was looking at Frankie. Jenny felt sorry for him. He didn't like school, so he didn't do well in school; nearly every night there was some kind of gruesome fuss over Frankie and school.

"What grade did you say you were in, Frankie?" Grandpa asked. He'd forgotten to take off his steel-rimmed glasses before supper, and they'd slipped down on his nose, giving him the look of an absent-minded tortoise.

"You know—tenth grade," Frankie mumbled.

"Next year," Mr. Pennoyer said, "he'll be in tenth grade again, if 'nothing' keeps on happening."

"But it's true, some days nothing happens in school," Jenny said.

"I never went past grade eight," Grandpa said. "Left school and went to work. My father, your grandfather, Frank, never got more than three grades of school."

"Times have changed, Pop," Mr. Pennoyer said. "Kids have to graduate these days. A boy can go to college if he puts his mind to it. Look at Vince."

"Vince, perfect Vince," Frankie said.

"Yeah, Vince," Mr. Pennoyer said. "You could take a few dozen lessons from your brother Vince, instead of giving out with the wise remarks."

"If we were all still living on the farm," Grandpa went on, "the boy could set his hand to work instead of school books."

"Frankie doesn't want to be a farmer," Mrs. Pennoyer said. She had Ethel next to her in the highchair and was feeding her from a dish of warmed baby food. "Besides, nobody's lived on the farm for years, Grandpa. If Frankie would just put more effort into his schoolwork he could do a whole lot better. We all know he's got the brains to do good work."

"Pennoyers grew up on the farm for six generations," Grandpa said, ignoring Mrs. Pennoyer's remarks. "My grandfather and my father grew up there. My great-great-great-grandfather cleared the first four acres of land in what was total wilderness. The land was covered solid with trees—"

"Okay, Pop, okay, we know all that."

"You've told us all that before, Grandpa," Gail said.

"So what?" Jenny said.

"So nothing. We've just heard it all before." Gail rolled her eyes ceilingward.

"Pennoyers kept clearing that land, till they had one hundred and ten acres cleared," Grandpa went on, emphasizing each word in his harsh voice. "My grandfather died working on the farm. But my father was a city man. So we had to rent it out after that. And it was rented till ten years ago."

"And it's just been hanging around ever since," Mr. Pennoyer interrupted. "Taking tax money down the drain, doing nobody any good. If you sold the place, Pop, you could probably make a nice few bucks on it. Money always comes in handy."

"I ain't selling it," Grandpa said. "I'm going back there sometime. See how things are. Why, that land could still be worked. That's rich, good farmland. All it needs is a little attention."

Mr. Pennoyer laughed. "You'll never go back, Pop." He brushed his hand over his thinning blond hair. "Quit dreaming. You've been talking that way all your life and never gone back yet."

Grandpa sat back in his chair. "I had some of the happiest times of my life at the farm. Summers my mother and I used to go by train from Alliance to Colfax, took us two days, and in Colfax we'd take a trolley to New Sayre. From there, we'd hire a carriage to take us the rest of the way, eight miles, to the farm. It's on a hill, the last farm on the road."

"Yes, Grandpa, we know," Mrs. Pennoyer said patiently.

"That road was Pennoyer Hill for the longest time. But after my grandmother began raising turkeys, the people around about there called it Turkey Hill. Those turkeys were something. My grandmother—"

"Oh, no, not here, not with that kind of talk," Mrs. Pennoyer said. "I don't want to hear about those turkey lice again, especially while I'm eating. No turkey lice!"

Grandpa raised a forkful of peas to his mouth and slowly chewed. Then he sipped his water. His mouth was clamped shut. He wasn't talking anymore.

Jenny's face flushed. Why couldn't they have listened just one more time? She knew Grandpa told his stories over and over, but so what? She'd heard the turkey story plenty of times. He liked telling it, and she liked listening to it! *My grandmother loved those turkeys like babies. Like little pets or children. Mornings, she'd sit on the back stoop in the sun and comb lice out of their feathers. She'd take a turkey into her lap, talk to it, and comb through the feathers like the pages of a book, taking out the lice and snapping each one on her fingernail. All night the turkeys slept in the trees and all day they ate grasshoppers, but every morning they waited around for Grandma to snap their lice.*

". . . traffic on Pittmann Street has just become worse and worse," Mrs. Pennoyer was saying. "Remember, Frank, when we moved here how quiet it was?"

"Wasn't quiet, ever," said Grandpa, contradicting her.

"Well, it was so," Mrs. Pennoyer said. "I know what I remember."

"Big trucks rumbling along the street at night, keep a person awake—"

"You wouldn't hear them, Pop, if you'd close your window," Mr. Pennoyer said.

"Always slept with my window open, and always will."

Mr. Pennoyer motioned Frankie to pass the biscuits. "Close your window, you'll sleep better, hear less noise—"

"Sleep with my window closed, feel like I'm in jail," Grandpa said thinly.

"—less noise and keep the damp out," Mr. Pennoyer went on, raising his voice. "You're damn stubborn, Pop. A man your age ought to have more sense!"

"How come you're always telling me to respect my elders?" Jenny broke in. "Grandpa's your elder, and that's not a very respectful way to—"

"You finished eating, big mouth?" her father said. "Well, finish up and be quiet."

Jenny plunged her fork viciously into a scrap of biscuit. Kill, kill. One law for *them,* another for kids. Out of the corner of her eye she saw her mother dab at Grandpa's chin with a napkin, saw Grandpa rear back like a horse that's been stung.

"Ketchup on your chin," Mrs. Pennoyer said. "I was just trying to be helpful. You're so touchy, Grandpa."

"Some people you can't help," Mr. Pennoyer said.

"Well, I can try," Mrs. Pennoyer said. "I'm not the

sort of person who can sit back and let things happen, no matter what."

Jenny felt that this was the prelude to something else. Her mother had a quivery, defiant expression at the corners of her mouth, the sort of expression she got when she was going to say something for someone's good.

"You all know what happened on this street last week," Mrs. Pennoyer said. "To poor Nicky Rimbaud. All week it's been on my mind. I can't forget his blood in the street."

Jenny stopped eating. She'd seen Nicky's blood on the street, too, the dark oily stain on the wet pavement. It had happened on a rainy afternoon. Coming home from school, she'd seen the ambulance angled in the road, red light flashing restlessly; a black police car fenced the street while a policeman wearing a wet white cape routed traffic toward Catherine Street. Jenny's first thought had been of Ethel. What if the baby had somehow freed herself from her playpen, bumped down the stairs, and with that pleased grin fixed on her fat red face crawled into the street? With that piercing thought, Jenny had run, and found Ethel safely in the playpen on the front porch. The crowd had gathered in front of the Rimbauds'.

"He walked right into the street," a woman said as the ambulance moved away, ghostly white in the blotchy rainfall, tires whispering over the wet pavement.

"Who?" Jenny said, touching the woman's arm.

"Nicky Rimbaud. You know, the retarded kid. This lousy traffic, the driver couldn't stop. His head split like an eggshell, it was so delicate."

Jenny had felt hollow. Nicky, strange, pitiful Nicky with his mild vacant eyes and huge, waterlogged head that lolled against his shoulder. The day before she had given him a handful of potato chips and he had droolingly smiled his thanks. She walked back home, feeling dazed and strange. Nicky. Poor Nicky. In her bedroom she'd walked around and around touching things, thinking, *Nicky's dead.* Not that she had ever loved Nicky, or even liked him that much. There had always been something faintly repulsive about him. But—dead? She picked up Ethel's Fuzzy from the crib, dropped it, moved a glass horse on Gail's gadget shelf, touched the snapshot of Grandpa tacked to the wall above her bed. Then she went to the window, pushed aside the curtain, frowning intently into the rain. Nicky had always been there on the street, strange and pitiable, but there. So this was the way things happened, she thought; so that was the way things changed.

"It might have been anyone," Mrs. Pennoyer said. "This traffic—I tell you, we're lucky no one in the family has been hurt. When I heard that screech of brakes that day my blood ran cold."

"Let's not talk about it now," Jenny said. "I don't want to think about Nicky dying."

"Who are you, the Queen of England?" Gail said. "Mom wants to talk about it."

"I'd rather talk about turkey lice than about Nicky being killed!"

"We have to talk about it," Mrs. Pennoyer said, "because it's a lesson to all of us, a warning."

"No use burying our heads in the sand," Mr. Pennoyer agreed. "It happened. Got to face reality, Jenny."

She pushed aside her plate. Reality. Nicky's head, eggshell frail, smashed. Oily smear of blood. Silent white ambulance. Mrs. Rimbaud crying high in her throat.

Mrs. Pennoyer poked a bit of mashed food into Ethel's mouth. "So, as I was about to say, I know, Grandpa, that you like to walk to that little tobacco store on Lyons Avenue, but ever since this awful thing happened to Nicky Rimbaud, I've been worrying and thinking about you. Now I spoke to Frank about this, and he agrees. We want you to promise us you won't cross the streets anymore without someone else with you. You know, to get to the tobacco shop you have to cross Pittmann at Fifth and then Collamer Avenue."

"You forgot Grove Avenue," Grandpa said shortly. "You forgot I might run in front of a car on Grove Avenue."

"Okay, Pop, okay, don't get on your high horse. Amelia's got a point. You're an old guy. Eighty-three years old. Hell, nobody expects you to be one hundred percent at your age. We've got to be careful, watch you, that's the long and short of it."

Grandpa pushed back his chair and fumbled in his sagging sweater pocket for his pipe. "That boy was retarded." Spots of brownish color appeared on his face. "Retarded and a child, may he rest in peace." His left hand began an aimless, agitated sweep of the table and knocked over a glass of water. The water spread over the tablecloth and the glass fell to the floor and broke.

"Wah, wah," Ethel said, pounding her fists on her highchair tray.

"For Christ sake, Pop," Mr. Pennoyer said. "I don't have enough broken stuff at the store, I have to come home and get the same thing!"

"Never mind," Mrs. Pennoyer said tightly, "it's only a glass. The children break glasses all the time."

Grandpa left the table, and after the glass was picked up, the rest of the family continued their meal. Jenny wanted to get away and go down to Grandpa, but knew better than to try before everyone had finished eating and the dishes were cleared, washed, and dried. It was her turn to help her mother in the kitchen.

"Will you switch kitchen nights with me?" she asked Gail.

"Why?"

"Because."

"That's no reason," Gail said, fingering the last piece of cake on the cake plate.

"Will you or won't you!"

"You are the rudest child I've ever had the misfortune of knowing," Gail said. She sliced a thin piece off the cake and delicately put it into her mouth.

"Then you won't?" Jenny said.

"You said it, I didn't." Gail put her dessert dish, sticky with crumbs, in front of Jenny. "Here, you might as well carry that in when you clear."

Jenny pushed back her chair. She felt her head blaze with anger at Gail and at all of them for the way they had acted toward Grandpa. She clanked dishes and silver and glasses together.

"Watch it," her mother said sharply. "I don't want any more broken dishes tonight."

In the kitchen her mother ran hot water in the sink and poured in detergent. "Finish clearing," she said, "and don't forget to wipe the table. And don't dawdle. I like these dishes wiped while they're still hot."

"Yes, yes, yes, okay," Jenny said. Her mother gave her an angry stare, and she subsided, doing her work silently and quickly, but the arguments in her head wouldn't subside.

"You and Dad talk to Grandpa like he's dumb. Or a kid," she said, grabbing a towel and starting to wipe dishes. "You make him feel awful."

Mrs. Pennoyer dipped a saucer in the rinse sink, then put it in the rubber drain. "Are you telling me how I should act? I've lived forty-three years, I guess I know how to act by now without my thirteen-year-old daughter advising me."

Jenny picked up a glass and rubbed it hard. "I just mean you should think more about Grandpa's feelings. He's a person, too."

"I know all about your grandfather, Jenny. I've lived with him under the same roof for thirteen years, and I knew him a long time before you were born.

Don't forget that. Let me tell you something, Jenny, it's no picnic living with that man. I don't like to say it, but that's the way it is. He's not the cleanest old man in the world, sometimes he doesn't change his underwear for a week. And his towels—when he finally brings them up to be laundered, I have to scrub them by hand. And I do! And the same stories over and over—when he gets going he doesn't give anyone a chance to get a word in edgewise." She scoured a pot fiercely.

Jenny concentrated on the glass she was drying. There was an aching tightness in her chest. "That's really a rotten way to talk about Grandpa."

"That's enough out of you. If you want to go to Rhoda's tomorrow night, you better watch your tongue right now."

"You don't want Grandpa to talk, you don't want him to do anything." Jenny knew she should stop, but couldn't. "You and Dad both, you act like you don't want Grandpa to even live."

"What a hateful way to talk! You ought to be slapped for talking that way about your parents. Apologize! You apologize to me at once."

For a moment Jenny couldn't speak; her throat was closed as tightly as a fist. "I'm sorry," she got out. "I'm sorry I said that."

Her mother's eyes held hers. Her mother had deep brown eyes, so brown that they seemed to spill over into the whites, which also had a faint tint of brown. "All right," she said at last, "I accept your apology. I try, you know, I don't want to hurt Grandpa. That's what I meant about the traffic. I just want him to be careful. Is that so hard to understand?" She looked at Jenny for a long time, holding her with her eyes. It was often like this after a fight. Her mother's eyes got deeper, browner, and she seemed to Jenny to be saying silently, *Please understand, don't hold it against me.* Jenny, in the grip of anger, hurt feelings, and outrage, would feel that plea, would be forced to meet

her mother's brown, pleading eyes, eyes that had soft-
ened and almost begged Jenny to understand. Understand what? It was always that nagging secret, that
feeling of something else behind the words they had
flung at each other.

# Chapter 5

"Here comes Ethel," Jenny sang out, carrying the baby into the kitchen on her hip the next morning. The Pennoyer family ate breakfast in the kitchen, rather than the dining room, and although it made for a crowded scene, it also made things cozy and warm. Breakfast was a good time of the day. Mrs. Pennoyer didn't mind making everyone a different breakfast (this morning they were having french toast, oatmeal, and scrambled eggs), and Ethel got passed from lap to lap, with everyone taking a turn squeezing her and feeding her from their plates.

"Look, Mom, Wilson's has a special on sweaters," Gail said, reading the newspaper over her father's shoulder.

"Maybe you can find something," Mrs. Pennoyer said. "You, too, Jenny."

"I'm going down right after school then," Gail said. "You want to come, brat?"

Jenny shook her head. "I'm going over to Rhoda's. Mom, can I sleep over at Rhoda's tonight? And eat supper with them?"

"Did they invite you?"

"Sure."

"Mrs. Rivers invited you?"

Jenny nodded and held her milk glass to Ethel's mouth. Ethel drank a little, then let the rest of the mouthful dribble down her chin. "Ethel, you slob," Jenny said.

"You sure it's all right with Mrs. Rivers?" Mrs.

Pennoyer said, heaping more oatmeal in Frankie's dish.

"Yes, Mom, positive."

"All right then."

"Thanks!" Jenny passed the baby to Gail. She wanted to get down to see Grandpa and tell him she wouldn't be home until tomorrow. She was stacking her knife and fork on her plate when Mr. Pennoyer groaned. "Oh, no. Look at this," he said, rattling the newspaper. "Would you believe it? They've got chuck down for thirty-nine cents a pound instead of ninety-three cents. I'm going to have every bargain-minded housewife in Alliance jamming the store. And when they find out it's a mistake they're all going to want to kill *me*."

"Maybe you could get the newspaper to send someone over to explain they made the mistake," Mrs. Pennoyer said.

"Sure, the mob'll string us both up together," Mr. Pennoyer said. "Oh, brother, this beats all."

"Poor Daddy," Jenny said, bringing her dishes to the sink.

"Jenny," her mother said, "write Rhoda's number down and tack it to the bulletin board." Mrs. Pennoyer glanced at the tackboard that hung on the wall behind the table and frowned. "What's that on the board anyway? Frankie, what's on the board?"

"I don't know," Frankie said, reaching behind him to pull down the piece of paper. "Oh, hey, it's from Grandpa," he said. "It says, 'To my family. From Carl Pennoyer. I am eighty-three, but not mentally retarded. I have crossed streets for at least seventy-eight of my years without assistance and without trouble. I have never once been struck by a car and killed. If I had been, I would certainly have a newspaper clipping to that effect.'"

"Jesus, that's all I need this morning," Mr. Pennoyer said. He took the piece of paper from Frankie's hand and read it over again. "I suppose Pop thinks that's funny." He looked around at the family. "Anyone here laughs, I'll crack him one. I swear, that'll be it."

Later when Jenny told Rhoda about the message on the bulletin board, they both got hysterical over it. "Your grandfather is the greatest," Rhoda said, still giggling. "I wish my grandfathers were like him, but ugh, they're both so dull. Grandfather Rivers spends all his time repairing watches, and Grandfather Herman won't even talk to me, hardly."

"He won't?" Jenny was shocked and slightly delighted at this further proof (as if she needed it) of Grandpa's uniqueness.

"Grandfather Herman says he never liked children and being old hasn't changed his opinion. Mother says never mind when I get to be about eighteen he'll be interested in me. That's when he got interested in her."

"Who can wait that long?" Jenny said. After eating supper at Rhoda's house, they'd gone out to Jericho Park, fooled around, racing up the footpaths and chinning themselves from a tree. Now they were returning to Rhoda's home.

"Hello," Rhoda called as they entered, "I'm back." She and Jenny went into the Rivers' living room where Mr. and Mrs. Rivers were watching TV.

"Well, look at her with her blouse hanging out," Mr. Rivers said. "Where has she been?"

"Your blouse hanging out like that doesn't look very nice, Rhoda," Mrs. Rivers said. She was a small woman with the same eager, interested face as her daughter. "Who have you been with, honey?"

"Nobody but Jenny," Rhoda said, tucking in her blouse.

"Look at her, destroying the evidence," Mr. Rivers teased. "I bet you were fooling around with a boy."

"No, I wasn't," Rhoda said. "You know I don't do that."

"We'll just have to ask Jenny," Mrs. Rivers said,

smiling and joining in the teasing. "Jenny will tell us the truth, won't you, Jenny?"

"We just walked around," Jenny said.

"Who'd you see?" Mrs. Rivers said. "Your boyfriend? Or was it Jenny's boyfriend?" She and Mr. Rivers both looked smilingly at Jenny. Jenny felt heat seeping into her face and neck.

"Now that you mention it," Mr. Rivers said, "seems to me Jenny Pennoyer's shirt is also sort of rucked out of her jeans. Now look at that, look at her hurrying to set herself right." Jenny felt her ears flaming. The Riverses were really nice, but they could always make her feel like a fool. She glanced at Rhoda, who was grinning. Rhoda was used to her parents.

"Where did you walk around?" Mr. Rivers said. He was a tall, big-bellied man.

"Jericho Park," Rhoda said.

"The park," Mr. Rivers said, turning serious. "Rhoda, how many times have Mother and I told you it's dangerous to go in the park after dark? There are all kinds of two-legged animals."

"It's not really dark out yet," Jenny said.

"Oh, yes it is," Mr. Rivers said. "I don't want you going in the park alone, Rhoda."

"I was with Jenny."

"Jenny is a wonderful girl, but she's not any protection for you, and you're not any protection for her."

"We're only thinking of you, honey." Mrs. Rivers patted Rhoda on the behind. "You girls go wash up; you look all flushed and hot. Then you can have some milk and cookies and go on to bed." She took one of Rhoda's hands. "Your nails need cutting, honey. And your hair, I'll have to trim your hair pretty soon; it's getting shaggy." She pulled Rhoda down to kiss her cheek. "Ummm, sweet! Oh, oh, is that a little pimpy I see developing on your chin? No picking now!"

The Riverses didn't yell and argue like the Pennoyers. Jenny had never heard either Mr. Rivers or Mrs. Rivers say a loud or harsh word to Rhoda. They had no children except Rhoda, and they seemed to enjoy nothing in life quite as much as Rhoda-watching.

"It would drive me bananas," Jenny said as they brushed their teeth in the Rivers' blue tile bathroom. (Mrs. Rivers had just popped her head in to check if Rhoda was wearing her flannel nightgown.)

Rhoda shrugged and examined her teeth in the bathroom mirror. "In one ear and out the other," she said. "That's my motto."

"Cool, you're really cool," Jenny said admiringly. "Me, I am hot as a firecracker. Do you think that's why we like each other? We're opposites, all right."

"Must be true love," Rhoda agreed.

In Rhoda's room they both got into the same twin bed to talk. "All this furniture in my room is bird's-eye maple," Rhoda said. She had twin maple beds with red and white striped spreads, matching curtains at the windows, a rag rug on the floor, a maple rocker, and a maple bureau cluttered with a camera, three bottles of cologne, a round-faced clock in a brushed red traveling case, a silver-backed brush, and four United Nations' dolls.

"You're supposed to be impressed when you hear bird's-eye maple," Rhoda said.

Jenny, who was indifferent to furniture, said, "Okay, I'm impressed. You know who'd appreciate this? Gail. She and my mother spend hours looking at the Sears catalogue. Gail wants my mother to promise to buy us new bedroom furniture for Christmas. Isn't that a rotten idea?"

"New furniture is nice," Rhoda said, spitting on her forefinger and rubbing a spot off the headboard. "I like new things."

"Some new things are all right. I wouldn't mind if I never had to wear any of Gail's clothes again. But furniture is different. You know my bureau at home? The one that's painted kind of an oceany green? That was my father's when he was a kid. I like it fine, but my mother says it's a piece of junk. So I'll probably have to have a new one whether I like it or not."

There was a knock at the door, and Mrs. Rivers came in. "Girls, don't forget you need your sleep. If you talk too late, you'll have bags under your eyes in the morning, Rhoda."

"We won't stay up long," Rhoda said. As soon as her mother shut the door, Rhoda turned on her side toward Jenny. "Let's talk real talk. Who do you love? Tell me his initials."

"C. P.," Jenny said.

"C. P.," Rhoda repeated. Then she got it. "Your grandfather. No fair. You know what I mean. What boy in school do you love?"

"How do you know I love anyone?"

"I know," Rhoda said. "I know! Listen, remember last term when I had a crush on Mr. Spencer? I told you, didn't I? And I told you about dreaming about your brother Vince."

"I never dream things like that," Jenny said, but instantly she remembered a dream she'd had only a few nights before about the boy whose name Rhoda was trying to get out of her. George Uhlmann. Old sexy George, with his slouching, easy walk. Passing him in the halls, Jenny couldn't help looking up, smiling hopefully, saying, Hiii! If she was lucky she got a distant smile out of George Uhlmann, the smile of a boy two years older than she, a boy who knew he was *something*.

"Give me his initials," Rhoda said. "Is he the same one as the summer?"

"Gawd, no!" All summer, out of boredom, Jenny had had a crush on Lloyd James, a boy who lived on Pittmann Street, who was her age but half a head shorter and filled with more pure male arrogance than even George Uhlmann. Lloyd wore his T-shirts with the sleeves cut off to show off his muscular arms. He was a weight lifter, he never acted small, and he never missed an opportunity to say something nasty to any girl who got near him. It had been so humiliating to have a crush on him. So stupid! Jenny had hated herself even as she made opportunities to bump into him. Thank goodness she was over that. "I hate Lloyd James," she said firmly. "I mean hate hate, not like hate."

"Thank goodness for that," Rhoda said. "I can't stand the slimy little beast. All right, give me a hint about the new one, his first initial is . . . ?"

"G.," Jenny said.

"G." Rhoda began reeling off all the boys in their class whose names began with G. "Gerald Whyken."

"No."

"Gary Bruno."

"No."

"George Taylor."

"No."

Jenny kept saying no, laughing harder and harder as Rhoda got more frustrated. "Come on, tell," Rhoda said, pinching Jenny's arm. "We're best friends, you have to tell me who he is." Rhoda didn't like being frustrated.

"Listen," Jenny said in a solemn voice, suppressing her laughter, "he's not in our class. He's older. And he's this fantastic sexy person who I thought I liked for a while, but now I'm getting to hate because he doesn't know I'm alive."

Rhoda pounced. "If you hate him, then it doesn't matter. Tell me his name."

"Initials, G.—" Jenny paused, drawing it out. "G.—U."

"G. U.," Rhoda repeated. "G. U., G. U., who do I know G. U.?" Then she screamed. "George Uhlmann. Oh, no, not George Uhlmann. Jenny, how could you. He's such a big snob!"

"You're right. A big snob, and a big conceited jerk. You know what? I'm not looking at him in the halls anymore. No more saying, Hi, George, hoping he'll deign to answer. No, sir! From now on when I see him, I cross my eyes."

Suddenly they were both giggling and clutching each other, arms around each other, face bursting laughter into face. "Jenny, I like you!" Rhoda cried, and hugging her tighter she kissed Jenny. They were both embarrassed. They drew apart, still smiling. Jenny saw Rhoda's face getting redder and redder. Jenny yawned elaborately. "Hey, maybe I better get into the other bed. Your mother will have kittens if she finds us still up." She crawled into the adjoining twin bed and punched the pillows to make it comfortable.

There was silence for a while. Then, "Jenny?"

"Yes?"

"You sleeping?"

"Not yet."

"Let's talk some more."

"Okay. What about?"

"Elephant jokes?"

"Oh, no!"

"Why do elephants wear pink tennis shoes?"

"Why? Why? I'm dying to know."

"Because white ones get dirty too fast. Okay, ready for the next one?"

"Never!"

"Why do elephants have wrinkled ankles?"

"I give up."

"Because their tennis shoes are laced up too tight."

Laughing, they rolled around in their beds. The embarrassment was over. Rhoda leaned across the space between the beds.

"Girls!" Mrs. Rivers called from the next room.

"Jenny," Rhoda whispered, "did I ever tell you I was a blue baby?"

"No," Jenny whispered back.

"I didn't have enough oxygen in my blood when I was born. I was literally blue, my mother says. I needed a complete transfusion. That's why no more babies after me, because my mother said she would never go through all that torture again."

"Rhoda," Jenny said, "when you get famous and write your autobiography you can call it, *I Was a Blue Baby, And I'm Still Blue, Baby!*"

"And she hates elephant jokes!"

Moments later, it was Jenny who broke the silence. "Rhoda, I was a birth-control baby."

"Birth-control baby? I never heard of that."

"The birth control my mother and father used didn't work, and the result was me."

"You mean you weren't wanted."

Jenny didn't answer. She hunched the covers over her shoulders. Rhoda leaned across the beds to touch Jenny's shoulder. "I'm sorry. I don't know why I said such a stupid thing."

Jenny lay still for a long time. Her thoughts drifted to her family . . . to Grandpa . . . to the strangeness of the way Rhoda lived, only one child watched over by two adults. Her throat felt dry and she thought about getting up for a drink. "Rhoda," she said softly, after a while. "Rhoda, you were right, anyway. I'm the family accident." Rhoda was sleeping already and didn't answer. Surprised at what she had said and yet, having said it, feeling as if she'd always known it, understanding now as if she'd always understood that plea in her mother's eyes, Jenny closed her eyes and went to sleep, too.

*Chapter 6*

One Saturday afternoon, only a month after he'd gone back to college, Vince walked in on the Pennoyer family. Jenny was in the kitchen cleaning up bowls and beaters after baking brownies. Mr. Pennoyer, who'd been laying new tarpaper on the garage roof, had just come in for a cup of coffee, and Mrs. Pennoyer was sitting at the table with him, showing him a sale in the Sears fall catalogue on an electric meat-slicing machine. "All chrome-plated steel construction," she read.

"How big is that blade?" Mr. Pennoyer said, and at that moment Vince entered.

"Greetings, family," he said as casually as if he came three hundred miles home from college every Saturday afternoon. He was wearing flared corduroy pants, a blue turtleneck shirt, and boots with brass studs on the straps. He'd let his hair and sideburns grow and looked, Jenny thought, fantastic. "Vince," she cried, throwing herself on his neck.

Mr. Pennoyer pushed back his chair. "Vince, hey, it's Vince." He embraced his son and stood back to look at him. "Did you get taller since the last time I saw you?"

Vince laughed. "No, Dad. But maybe you got shorter."

"Hey, you're still a fresh kid," Mr. Pennoyer said, smiling. "What are you doing here anyway? Are you hungry? Sit down, have something to eat. Jenny, give

Vince some brownies. Amelia, warm up that stew from last night."

Vince rubbed his hand over his thick dark mustache. He was a good head taller than his father, wiry and handsome. "I ate already, Dad, grabbed something at a diner on the road. So how are you, Dad? You look great." He rubbed Jenny's head. "Where's my other cute little sisters?" He bent over his mother. "How are you, Mom? You okay? Feeling okay?" He kissed his mother on the cheek.

Mrs. Pennoyer held on to Vince's hand, half smiling, half frowning. "Vince, what is it? Why'd you come home like this so suddenly, without warning? I just got a letter from you a week ago and you didn't say anything about coming home. Aren't you supposed to be in school?"

"Well—I brought you home a surprise."

"A surprise?" Mrs. Pennoyer said. "What kind of surprise? Vince, I hope you didn't spend any money—"

Vince laughed. "It's a nice surprise. I hope you think it's as nice as I think it is." He went to the door and called. "Okay, surprise, you can come in now."

"What is this?" Mr. Pennoyer said, just as a blonde girl holding a package wrapped in gold tissue paper came to the kitchen door. Vince put his arm around her. "This is Valerie," he said.

"Hi, everybody," Valerie said.

"That's your surprise?" Mrs. Pennoyer's face wore a faintly irritated expression.

"Hi, Valerie," Jenny said.

Valerie stuck out her free hand to Jenny. "I bet you're—no, not Gail. You're Jenny. Am I right?" She had her silky hair pulled into two long straight ponytails and was wearing a nubby peach sweater that Jenny recognized as one of Vince's. "Vince told me about you and about everyone in the family," Valerie went on. "I'm so glad to meet you, and you, Mrs. Pennoyer. And you, too, Mr. Pennoyer. It sounds trite, but I honestly feel as if I know you all already." She had a charming smile.

"When Vince said a surprise, I thought you might be a strawberry shortcake," Jenny said. "Or maybe I just hoped you would be."

Valerie laughed. "She's better than strawberry shortcake," Vince said.

"Do you go to college with Vince?" Mrs. Pennoyer broke in. "Is that where you met?"

"Yes, I'm an art major. I'm going to be an art teacher on the elementary level. I think little kids do such marvelous spontaneous stuff in art. I want to get them when they're young and fresh."

"Isn't she beautiful, isn't she great?" Vince said. He had brought home other girls many times, but Jenny had never seen him act quite so proud and excited.

Mr. Pennoyer cleared his throat loudly. "Sit down, kids, sit down. Here—uh—Virginia, take a seat. Amelia, give the kids a soda."

"I really don't want anything right now, Mr. Pennoyer, thanks anyway," Valerie said, seating herself at the table. She put the gift-wrapped package down in front of her. "My name is *Valerie*," she added.

Jenny leaned forward to look at Valerie's rings. One had a streaked, lumpy orange stone, another contained several tiny green stones, and a third silver band was made in the shape of two clasped hands.

"I love your friendship ring," Jenny said.

"It's not exactly—" Valerie broke off, smiled, and smoothed the gold tissue-wrapped package.

"Don't you young people have to be back in school Monday morning?" Mrs. Pennoyer said. She looked at the clock over the stove. "You've made an awfully long trip for just a few hours' visit. You'll have to start back first thing tomorrow morning. I don't think you were very practical, Vince."

"'Aren't you glad to see me, Mom? Didn't you miss me? Your favorite son." Standing behind Valerie, his hands on her shoulders, Vince had a special, teasing grin on his face, the smile Jenny thought of as the Vince-grin. He could almost always get anything he wanted with the Vince-grin.

"Of course I like seeing you," Mrs. Pennoyer said. "But all that driving—you should be studying over the weekend."

"How's the car holding up?" Mr. Pennoyer said. They had given Vince a 1970 Dodge Dart as a high school graduation present. "You taking care of it, Vince?"

"The car is okay," Vince said. "Listen, I've got something to tell you two. I didn't come all this way home just to say hello or talk about the car."

Mr. and Mrs. Pennoyer exchanged a glance. "All right, out with it," Mr. Pennoyer said.

Vince smoothed down his mustache, but didn't say anything. The room got very quiet. Jenny could hear the electric clock buzzing, the refrigerator humming, and in the cellar the bell that signaled the end of the washer's cycle rang. "Go on, tell," Valerie said, looking up at Vince.

"Well, listen . . . well, Val and I . . . actually, we're married."

Valerie shifted the gift package on the table and nodded. "Yes, we are," she said.

"That's my surprise, our surprise," Vince said. "We got married two days ago."

"Then that's your wedding ring!" Jenny said, and Mr. Pennoyer half stood up, while Mrs. Pennoyer simply stared, her face going white.

"Repeat that," Mr. Pennoyer said.

"We're married, Dad." Now Vince spoke very fast. "We'd been talking about it and thinking about it, and we decided—let's do it, what are we waiting for?"

"So you decided just like that," Mr. Pennoyer said. "It was something to do over a weekend!"

Mrs. Pennoyer went to the sink and ran water into the electric coffeepot. "I'm in a state of shock," she said. The water overflowed, and she turned off the faucet. "I thought when you brought her in and said you had something to tell us—I guessed you were engaged. But this—I never even heard you mention her, Vince!"

"We knew each other last year," Vince said. "I must have mentioned Valerie to you, Mom. Didn't I? Sure, I must have."

"I think I remember hearing her name in a letter," Jenny said.

Mrs. Pennoyer, holding the dripping coffeepot, turned to Valerie. "What's your name? Valerie what?"

Smiling faintly, Valerie said, "Valerie Pennoyer."

It gave Jenny a queer shock to realize that this thin blonde girl now had the same name as she did, now was part of the Pennoyer family.

"Your parents—do they know you're married?" Mrs. Pennoyer said. "Have you notified them?" She measured coffee out of the tin into the aluminum basket, spilling some on the counter. "Do your parents approve of what you've done? Just running off and getting married without a word to anyone? I can't imagine they're happy about that!"

"To be truthful, they're upset," Valerie said. "That's why we came to you. Vince said—"

"Vince," Mr. Pennoyer interrupted, "why didn't you talk this over with me before you did such a stupid thing? Why didn't you ask me what I thought? I would have told you—"

"I knew what you'd say," Vince said.

"Oh, you did!"

"Yes, I did."

They stared at each other. Jenny nibbled a brownie nervously.

"Frank—" Mrs. Pennoyer said.

Vince put out his hand toward his father. "You may as well know everything. I've dropped out of school."

"You've left school, Vince," Mrs. Pennoyer said. "Oh, Vince! How could you?"

"It's only temporary. Now, listen, Mom—"

"Dropped out of school," Mr. Pennoyer repeated. He sat back heavily in his chair. "Dropped out of school! Okay, let's have it all." He looked over at Valerie. "Is she pregnant?"

"Oh, no," Valerie said. "No, Mr. Pennoyer, we're not that naive. Nothing like that."

"Naive," Mrs. Pennoyer said. "Is that what you kids call it now?"

"Take it easy, Mom," Vince said. "Let me explain this. We've both dropped out. Val's family told her if she got married, no more money. So that explains her dropping out."

"And what explains your dropping out?" Mr. Pennoyer said. "You lost your interest in getting somewhere in the world?"

"I don't want my wife working at some crummy job while I'm in school," Vince said. "We figured if we can live here at home, we'll both work, we'll save our dollars and then go back to school next year."

"How can you be so dumb?" Mr. Pennoyer banged his hand on the table. "I want you to stay in school! You don't have to drop out because she does. That's her problem!"

"Dad, I just told you—"

"I heard you, damn it!"

"Frank, don't get upset," Mrs. Pennoyer said. "You're shouting. There's no need to shout."

Mr. Pennoyer tugged at the collar of his flannel shirt. "Okay, okay, I'm calm. Now listen to me, Vince, you think you'll go back to college, but you don't know what you're talking about. You've got everything ass backward. Things happen—"

"Dad, we've figured—"

"Vince, I know!" Mr. Pennoyer raised his voice. "Kids have big plans, but nature gets in the way." He pointed a finger at Valerie. "Before you turn around she'll have a baby and that'll be the end of all your fine plans."

"No, Mr. Pennoyer, that isn't going to happen to us." Valerie put the gift-wrapped package on her lap and fussed with the ribbon, smoothing it out. "Definitely not."

"Babies come," Mr. Pennoyer said. "You ever heard that saying, the best laid plans of mice and men? Babies will knock all your plans into a cocked hat! They come whether you want them or not! Amelia, tell this son of yours I've been working my head off for him for years, and now he wants to throw it all away like it's nothing."

"Are you going to kick us out, Dad?" Vince said. "Are you going to tell me to go live someplace else? Because if that's what you want, it's okay with me!"

"Now, Vince," Mrs. Pennoyer said. "We're not going to turn our backs on you. Calm down. Your father just got upset. Frank, tell Vince we're not turning our backs on him."

Mr. Pennoyer drummed his fingers on the table. "I'm not taking back anything I said, but you're my son, and that means I stick by you no matter what you've done."

"I haven't committed a crime, Dad."

There was a tense silence. Mrs. Pennoyer poured herself a cup of coffee, then sat down. Jenny brushed brownie crumbs off the table. Valerie cleared her throat. "Mrs. Pennoyer—" She pushed the wrapped box toward Mrs. Pennoyer. "This is a present for you and your family from your new daughter-in-law."

Mrs. Pennoyer looked at the box. "Really, you shouldn't have—"

"Open it, Mom," Jenny said.

Mrs. Pennoyer pulled off the ribbon, wound it neatly, then carefully unwrapped the gold paper. "Such nice wrappings," she murmured. Jenny leaned forward. Mrs. Pennoyer folded the tissue paper, smoothing it out, put the ribbon on top, then opened the box and looked inside. "Oh, my," she said, lifting out a narrow blue plastic container with gold lettering across the bottom. "An electric toothbrush," Mrs. Pennoyer said. She lifted off the container cover to disclose the blue plastic electric brush holder and four tiny toothbrushes, each a different color and each sealed in clear plastic.

"An electric what?" Mr. Pennoyer said. "What the hell kind of present is that?"

Valerie's lips pinched together. "I thought you'd like it."

"Where'd you get that idea?"

"Don't be so rough, Dad!"

"My parents have one," Valerie said. "They like it. They said they didn't even realize they were brushing all wrong till they got it."

Mr. Pennoyer tapped his two large front teeth. "The day I get too old or too lazy to hold my own toothbrush and swish it back and forth on my teeth a few times you can take me to the old peoples' home and leave me there. Amelia, you got that? The old folks' home!" His voice was loud and angry, and Jenny felt sorry for Vince and Valerie, being on the receiving end of all that anger. All they'd done was fall in love and get married. She was impressed, though, with the way Valerie was taking her father's temper. She sat there, not saying a word, smiling faintly, altogether cool as a cucumber.

## *Chapter 7*

"The love birds are sleeping on the couch," Jenny told
Rhoda while hashing over the brand-new situation in
the Pennoyer household.

"Is it one of those couches that pull out into a bed?"
Rhoda asked. There was an envious note in her voice.
"Your family is cool. Nothing like that could ever
happen in my family."

"The whole house is a disaster area," Jenny said.
"Wait till you see it, you won't recognize it."

The Pennoyer living room had always been a cozy
place, stuffed with upholstered chairs, side tables,
lamps, Mrs. Pennoyer's upright piano, and a big soft-
looking couch. There were red curtains at the windows and bright red velvet pillows with tassels on
either end of the couch. Clay pots of ferns and other
green plants were crowded on a heavy mahogany table
sitting in the bay window that faced the street. The
room had always been a family gathering place. Jenny
and Gail did their homework in there; Mrs. Pennoyer
picked out her odd tunes on the piano; everyone
watched TV. But with Vince and Valerie sleeping on
the couch, the room no longer belonged to the family.

Sometimes now, Jenny reported, the couch wasn't
cleared of blankets and sheets until nearly time for it
to be made into a bed again. There were overflowing
suitcases and duffel bags on the chairs, shoes, boots,
and sneakers everywhere, sweaters flung on the piano,
and Vince's sweat socks in odd places collecting dust-
balls. On top of the TV were tissues, brushes, combs,

keys, and a collection of pink, yellow, and green plastic bottles containing variously Vince's hair lotion and deodorant, and Valerie's hand cream and lemon-scented cologne.

Books were stacked haphazardly in piles on the floor, there were two tennis rackets leaning in a corner, suitcases on the piano bench, and Valerie's collection of stuffed plush cats (which she'd had since childhood) regarded the family with glassy-eyed indifference from the top of the couch.

"Stuffed cats," Jenny said, "like Ethel's 'Fuzzy.' I thought when you got married you grew up and forgot all that stuff."

"Oh, I don't know, I can see saving favorite things," Rhoda said. She slept with a worn white stuffed dog every night. "Valerie sounds nice."

"She's all right," Jenny said neutrally. The truth was she hadn't made up her mind about Valerie yet. Sometimes she liked her, sometimes she didn't. "We're all ready to kill her in the mornings, I can tell you that, Rhoda." Valerie was an early riser and a bathroom hog. Although she wasn't yet working, she got up when everyone else did, and four mornings out of five managed to slither into the bathroom before anyone else. But instead of whisking through her morning clean-up and getting out, she took a long shower without which, she said, she couldn't face the day.

"What's she got to face, that's what I want to know," Jenny said. "Me, I've got to face teachers. Dad has to face customers, and Mom has to face dishes and diapers."

"You're just having trouble getting adjusted to someone else in your house," Rhoda said wisely.

"You should hear what goes on now in the morning. Talk about yelling and screaming. This morning Frankie and I collided on the stairs going down to Grandpa's apartment. We each had the same brainstorm at the same time, to use Grandpa's toilet and sink. Poor Grandpa. I don't think he knew what hit him when we came flying in like that."

"It sounds like fun to me," Rhoda said.

"You're nuts, you know that," Jenny said. "It's only fun when you see something like that on TV. And it isn't only mornings. Dinnertime with all of us crowded around the table, all squeezed together, with all those elbows and hands and gimmee and grabbing and all those dishes and silverware and bowls of food—it's too much!"

"Well, it's probably only for a little while," Rhoda said. "They'll get their own place, won't they?"

Jenny shook her head. "No, that would be stupid. They have to save money, that's the whole point of being home. As soon as Valerie gets a job, they'll be banking two paychecks."

Vince had gone to work almost immediately in the Big K where Mr. Pennoyer was assistant manager. Every morning and night Valerie read the want ads and whenever a job sounded like a good possibility she followed up on it. The rest of the time she hung around the house eating fruit and drinking tea, taking all of Vince's pictures out of the family photo albums, and listening to music, plugged in with earphones to Vince's tape deck. At intervals she made forays into the bathroom and the kitchen, leaving behind her a scattered trail of crumpled, perfumed tissues, stained teacups balancing precariously in odd places, and fruit pits wrapped neatly in napkins.

"*Why* do you do this?" Jenny asked one Saturday morning, pointing to one of Valerie's napkin-wrapped fruit pits.

"Do what?" Valerie was sitting at the kitchen table with a cup of tea, a book propped open in front of her, while Jenny did the morning dishes before going out for a walk with Grandpa.

"Wrap fruit pits up like presents," Jenny said.

"Do I do that?" Valerie laughed. "That's cute of me."

"It's weirdo," Jenny said. "Why can't you just throw them in the garbage, bare?"

"Oh, Jenny, now don't try to make a big Freudian thing out of this," Valerie said. "We all have our little funny-farm habits. What's yours?"

"I'm normal," Jenny said. "No vices. Don't smoke dope, don't swear, don't cheat on tests at school."

"Dull, dull, dull," Valerie teased. "I recommend you take up wrapping fruit pits in napkins."

That was one of the times, Jenny told Rhoda, when she actually liked her sister-in-law. Other times she wasn't so sure—there was something very cool and a little bit hidden about Valerie. Or so she thought, anyway. Vince, obviously, didn't share her opinion, and her mother seemed to have become quite fond of Valerie. In fact, it was her mother who was most embarrassed by the lack of privacy Vince and Valerie had to suffer. That was why she kept changing things. That was why Frankie had to switch places with Vince and Valerie. He got the living room, and they got his bedroom, complete with bureau, posters, and bunk beds.

"Bunk beds," Vince said at breakfast. "Bunk beds! Ye gads, I haven't had to sleep in a bunk bed since I went to camp the summer I was ten. I'm a married man now."

"We tried sleeping on one of them together," Valerie said, "but it doesn't work. They're so narrow, they aren't made for two people."

"Who gets the bottom bunk?" Gail asked.

"We take turns," Valerie said, making a face.

The duffels, sweat socks, stuffed cats, and plastic bottles were now distributed around Frankie's room, but the family was still not in possession of the living room. Now it was Frankie's room and he showed no inclinations to share it with anyone. He left his jeans and underwear in the middle of the rug or hanging from a lamp, argued with everyone about which TV shows they could watch, and infuriated his father by asking him not to smoke in there, as the fumes were bad for his lungs, which he meant to keep in good shape for running.

No one was terribly satisfied with the way things were, and gradually everyone became more than a little edgy. One morning Gail was practically in tears because Valerie had kept the bathroom so long that Gail hadn't had time to put on the eye shadow she could apply only under the bright bathroom light.

"Sorry, sorry, sorry," Valerie said, sweeping out in a white terrycloth robe, her hair turbaned up in a towel. She gave Gail a hug. "Anyway, you don't need make-up on your eyes."

"Yes, I *do*. My eyes look *naked* without it. Why can't you get up later!"

"I believe in getting up with my husband," Valerie said. "I told you I was sorry!"

That same night, Vince and Mr. Pennoyer got into a heated argument over a mistake Vince had made at work. Grandpa tried to conciliate and was told by Mr. Pennoyer to butt out, and Jenny, leaping to her grandfather's defense, was called a big mouth and sent from the table. Furiously, she took her plate into the kitchen and swept the contents into the garbage pail.

"I don't know what's the matter with this family," she heard her mother say. "It's one uproar after another."

It sure is, Jenny agreed silently. She leaned against the kitchen counter, listening to the voices, the clatter of silver and dishes, and Ethel banging on her highchair tray.

"Stepping on each other's feet day and night," Mrs. Pennoyer went on. "The house is a mess all the time. I feel like I'm living in the eye of a hurricane."

"That's the calm place, Ma," Vince said.

"Well, you know what I mean! Everything's upside down. I'm getting so nervous I don't know how much longer I can take this."

"I don't like that," Mr. Pennoyer said. "Amelia, you've got to take it easier—"

"It's all my fault," Valerie said. "Mine and Vince's."
It was a humble-sounding statement, but Jenny, peering in from the kitchen, saw that Valerie didn't look at all humble. Thoughtful, maybe. Determined, maybe. But humble? No!

"There must be some better way to work things out," Valerie said.

"I wish there was," Mrs. Pennoyer said, "but I haven't been able to think of it."

## Chapter 8

"What are you doing down here?" Jenny said. Coming home from school, she'd discovered Valerie in Grandpa's apartment. "Where's Grandpa?"

"Your grandfather's gone for a walk, Jenny." Standing in the middle of the room, Valerie had her hands in the pockets of her slacks. "I'm just looking around here, thinking about things. You know, this is potentially a darling little place. Really cute."

"Cute," Jenny said. There was nothing cute about Grandpa, and there was nothing cute about the way he lived.

"The paint is old and scrungy-looking now," Valerie said, "but that's nothing. Fresh paint is easy and would do miracles here." She paced off the floor. "And a nice bright linoleum—" She went into the cubicle and flushed the toilet. "Something could be done here, too," she called to Jenny. "A bright yellow gloss on the walls to add light, and a fluffy cover on the throne seat in—oh, raspberry, or some other really warm shade. And a picture on the wall."

Jenny stood at the door of the cubicle. "Pictures on the john wall. Who'd want that?"

Valerie put up her hands like a frame. "Me! It would be something different. Maybe even this whole wall full of stuff—cartoons and line drawings, that sort of thing. I like that, Jenny. The flush box in the middle of art work. It's a giggle." She pushed past Jenny. "Also this entire place is crying out for plants, especially that window." She pointed to the street level window above the metal table. "That window really knocks me out. It's great, and totally neglected. Geraniums in the window boxes, masses of them. Don't you think so, Jenny?"

"Grandpa likes things plain, just the way they are," Jenny said. She took the deck of cards from the sideboard, sat down at the table, and laid out a game of solitaire. "Anyway, why are you bothering to figure all this out? Grandpa won't change anything. It's been just like this ever since I can remember."

"I'll let you in on a little secret," Valerie said. "Want to hear?"

Jenny looked up from her card game. "Sure."

"I think this apartment would be perfect for Vince and me," Valerie said. "In the middle of the night last night I woke up and realized this was the perfect solution."

Jenny stared at her sister-in-law. It was strange— Valerie was speaking plainly, but for a moment Jenny couldn't relate the sounds to any sense. Then she shook her head, as if clearing her ears of water. "Where would Grandpa go?" she said.

"Listen, this is the beautiful part of it," Valerie said. "There's a place for everyone. Vince and I will come down here, and your grandfather will go upstairs with Frankie."

"Grandpa with Frankie?" Jenny saw that she was losing at solitaire and gathered up the cards. "I think the whole idea is crazy," she said.

Valerie's eyes narrowed. "Why don't you go out and play?" she said. "Your grandfather probably won't be back for a while."

"I'll wait for him." Jenny laid out the cards again and put a red queen on a black king.

Valerie wandered around the apartment, touching things, and humming under her breath. "I'm really surprised at your parents letting your grandfather live alone down here," she said. She kicked lightly at one of the stacks of yellowed newspaper piled against the wall. "That's a fire hazard, a real fire hazard." She opened a drawer in the sideboard and poked among the things there. "He's got so much old junk—"

"That's a private drawer!" Jenny said.

Valerie closed the drawer. "You're a regular little mother hen about your grandfather, aren't you? I notice at the dinner table how you're always watching him, picking up his fork if he drops it, stuff like that."

Jenny slapped down a card, black two on red three. Hold out the ace of hearts. She watched Valerie looking with that measuring look in her eyes. How had she ever thought she liked Valerie? Now she didn't like her at all. No, not at all! Valerie was small boned, short, almost frail looking, but Jenny sensed now that there was something strong as steel inside her. Well, I'm strong, too, Jenny thought, and so is Grandpa. Absently she put a red ten on a black jack. She'd never thought of herself as strong before and suddenly had an image of herself with a lance taller than she, barring the way to Grandpa's apartment while Valerie and Vince futilely tried to get past her. Past her? Muscles Pennoyer? She giggled.

"What's so funny?" Valerie said.

"Nothing," Jenny said.

"I don't like that sarcastic smile," Valerie said. "I thought I could count on you, Jenny."

"Count on me—for what?"

"To be somebody with some understanding," Valerie said. "The rest of this family—" She tossed the two heavy ponytails she wore over her shoulders. "Well, except for Vince, of course—oh, never mind. But I'm going to speak to your father about this apartment," she said, going to the door. "I'm going to speak to him tonight."

Later that evening, Mr. and Mrs. Pennoyer and Vince and Valerie all started down to Grandpa's apartment. Jenny, who had been halfheartedly doing her homework, pushed aside her books and ran to join them.

"Go finish your homework," her mother said. "You're not needed down here."

"I'm done," Jenny said, quickly crossing her fingers behind her back. Childish, but necessary, she felt. Four against one. Grandpa would need her to even things up a bit.

Her father rapped on Grandpa's door, then opened it. Grandpa was sitting by his old American Bosch radio, his ear bent to the cloth-covered speaker.

"Pop, we've got something to talk to you about," Mr. Pennoyer said as they all crowded into the little room. "Can we sit down?"

"Sit down, make yourselves comfortable," Grandpa said, getting up and clearing a couple of chairs. "What can I do to help you?"

Mr. Pennoyer lit a cigarette. "Valerie here has come up with a good idea," he said. "You know the way we're all overcrowded upstairs. Well, Valerie has figured out a way to ease the situation. Now I want you to listen and consider, Pop, before you say anything. I want you to try to look at it from every angle."

"Get to the point, Frank," Grandpa said.

Mr. Pennoyer's scalp flushed. "The idea is for you to come live upstairs, share Frankie's room, and let the young couple live down here."

"I don't want to live upstairs," Grandpa said. "I get along fine on my own, minding my own business."

"This is a *good* idea Valerie has had," Mrs. Pennoyer said, pulling down the sleeves of her sweater. "We're in such a mess upstairs, and this would solve everything. The young people need their privacy, their own kitchen, their own bathroom. You know how important that is for young folks, Grandpa." She spoke softly, but distinctly, leaning toward Grandpa.

"You wouldn't like it down here," Jenny said to Valerie. "You think it's cute now, but everybody's upstairs tramping over your head, making noise all the time—"

"I wouldn't mind," Valerie said. "I'm very noise-tolerant. Anyway, it couldn't be any noisier than being right in the house with all of you." She put her hand on the back of Vince's neck. "Right, honey?"

"It's dark down here," Jenny said. "Especially in winter. And damp. You'd need at least three sweaters to keep yourself warm. And something else, there's no shower. What about that? *You* have to have a shower."

"Jenny," her father said, "will you butt out?"

"Val can go upstairs and shower," Vince said. "No sweat."

"I see you've thought of everything," Grandpa said.

"You have to admit it's a practical suggestion," Mr. Pennoyer said. "The more I think about it, the better it seems. Realistically, Pop, we all know you don't keep up this apartment. Take the walls, they ought to be washed down and painted. It's too much for you, and I'm busy, so it doesn't get done. Things are going downhill here."

"Upstairs with us, Grandpa, you'd have everything you need," Mrs. Pennoyer said. "You'd be right there with all of us watching out for you."

Grandpa reached for his aspirin bottle and shook two of the tablets into the palm of his hand.

"What do you say, Pop? It's not forever. It would only be for a year, and then the kids are going back to college. Letting them live here would be something you could do for all of us."

"It would be an unselfish and generous thing," Mrs. Pennoyer agreed.

Grandpa looked as if he were biting a lemon. "I can't do that," he said. "If I could help any other way—" He picked up a newspaper from one of the stacks. "Here's a newspaper ten years old, Vincent. Are you studying history? These newspapers could be very helpful to you. Come down and read them whenever you want to."

Vince shook his head. "I'm not doing much reading these days, Grandpa."

"Then I guess I can't help you," the old man said.

# Chapter 9

Outside it was dark. The window above Grandpa's metal table was slightly open, and sounds floated in. Cars sent showers of pebbles flying from the recently tarred road. A gray cat, tail high, came to the window, sniffed, then passed on. A man walked by; Jenny saw the bottom of his trousers, frayed and muddy, and his heavy boots with worn-down heels.

Grandpa was chewing aspirin, the bottle sitting on the table next to a chipped yellow cup half filled with sugar. Twice in the past week Jenny had caught Grandpa sitting at his table with the lights off, just sitting there, his hands absently fumbling at the buttons on his saggy-pocketed sweater. "What are you doing?" she asked the last time.

"Thinking," he'd said.

"Thinking about what?"

"Things." And that was all he would say. But she knew he was thinking about Valerie and Vince wanting his apartment for themselves. He'd said no, sorry no, but her parents weren't taking no for an answer. Both her father and her mother had come downstairs several times to talk to Grandpa again quietly and seriously. Gail had been up and down, too, getting ready for the party she was giving in the other side of the cellar. The whole thing made Jenny sick. Why didn't they all stay upstairs where they belonged?

Now she went to the sideboard and took out the deck of cards and sat down opposite Grandpa at the table. "Let's play cards."

"Cards?" His eyes focused on her.

"Unless you want to sit here thinking some more."

"Eh," he said in disgust. "Thinking. What's the stakes?"

"Quarter of a penny a point." She shuffled the limp cards, rippling them together, then breaking them apart for another shuffle. Footsteps pounded down the cellar steps outside Grandpa's apartment. "Play this record," a boy's voice said, coming clearly through the wall.

"Who's that?" Grandpa said.

"Gail's having a party. I thought I told you."

A moment later music filled the air, the heavy beat of a drum and a girl singing about love in faraway places. There were more steps, voices, and laughter.

Jenny turned up the top card. "The party was Valerie's idea. Gail lost two pounds sticking to a diet Valerie gave her, and Valerie said she ought to reward herself with a party. And Mom and Dad are out tonight, so they both thought it would be a perfect night."

Grandpa held the cards close to his nose. "You didn't shuffle these cards very good."

"You always say that." The top card was a three of hearts. "You want that?"

"I'm thinking it over," he said loftily. He studied his hand, studied the top card, then shook his head. "I don't want it. I suppose you do."

Jenny took the three of hearts, fitting it into her hand. She laid down a jack of clubs. Grandpa moaned in mock anguish. "You dealt me the worst cards in the deck."

In the other part of the cellar the noise was escalating—the heavy pounding beat of the music, shrieks, and laughter, all of it mixed with loud thumps against the wall. Jenny and Grandpa played several hands, all of which Grandpa lost. "You're not paying attention," Jenny scolded. Her foot beat in time to the music pouring in through the thin walls.

"That racket is distracting me," Grandpa said, putting down his cards. "I've had enough of this. What do I owe you? Add it up." He got up and lit the fire under the tea kettle on the stove. "You want some tea, child?"

"Sure," she said, biting the end of the pencil. "Grandpa, you owe me twenty-five cents. How about that?" Smiling, she looked over at him, but he didn't seem to hear her. His eyes were focused inward.

"Well, Jenny," he said, coming back to the table and slowly lowering himself into his chair, "should I do it? Should I give Vincent and his wife my apartment? Your father has got me more than half convinced I'm a selfish old fool."

"You're not!" Jenny's face heated. "You're not selfish, don't let them talk that way to you." She jumped up and hugged him around the neck. "Why'd they have to come home, just to make trouble?"

He unwound her arms. "They're doing what they have to do. Young people have to get together, get married, have a place to live—"

"That's all right," she said fiercely, "but this is your place!"

"My place," he said. "My place. Well, is it my place? Or is it your father's?" The music rose louder than ever on the other side of the wall, and he reached for his aspirin bottle. He put two more tablets in his mouth and chewed them. His hands shook clumsily as he recapped the bottle. Again the volume of the music soared and waves of sound reverberated through the apartment. "Are they all deaf out there?" Grandpa said. His mouth was thin. "Crazy kids, what are they doing down here anyway?" Spots of color came to his cheeks. Jenny saw how agitated he was—not about the kids and the music, really, but the apartment and the pressure on him to give it up. "Turn the damn noise off," he shouted, but the music, laughter, and thumps on the wall continued as before. He half rose.

"Wait, Grandpa, I'll go out there and get them to

be quieter," Jenny said. "You stay here. Don't yell, Grandpa, I'll tell them." She slipped out of Grandpa's door, closing it carefully behind her, and into the cellar, which Gail and Valerie had spent the afternoon decorating with balloons and twists of crepe paper.

Gail had invited about a dozen of her friends. On a card table were two huge bowls of popcorn and several large bottles of soda. Gail's best friend, Francine Jones, was doing handstands against the wall of Grandpa's apartment. *Thump! Thump!* Francine's feet hit the wall, her skirt covered her face, and her bright yellow panties showed. Gail was dancing with Wally Franklin who had taken off his shirt and was bare-chested.

"What are you doing here?" Gail said, noticing Jenny. "I told you this party was private."

"Wild party," Jenny said.

"Whoop-ee-do," Gail said in a bored voice.

"It's too noisy for Grandpa."

"You joining the party?" Wally asked.

"Not her," Gail was emphatic.

To annoy Gail, Jenny said, "I'll come if I want to."

"Oh, no, you won't!"

"It's a free country."

"Hooray for freedom," Wally said.

"How come you're not wearing your shirt?" Jenny said. Wally grinned. He had little red pimples on his forehead.

"He's showing off his wonderful body, child," Gail said.

*Thump! Thump!* Francine did another handstand. At the same time, a girl shrieked, "The pig spilled Coke down the front of my blouse!"

Jenny shook Gail's arm. "You better get them to keep it down. Grandpa is real nervous."

"What do you mean Grandpa is nervous? Tell him to take a tranquilizer if he's so nervous."

"Gail, don't be a pig! Just get everyone to keep it down, okay?"

"It certainly isn't okay," Gail said. "Who do you

think you are, barging into my party and telling me how to run it? My friends are just having f—"

An angry voice interrupted, "Turn that racket down!" It was Grandpa, angrily stomping over to the record player and yanking the cord out of the wall. In the sudden silence, Francine remained standing on her hands. "Get your feet off the wall, you ridiculous child," Grandpa said.

A wave of laughter swept the room. Several of the boys began jeering at Grandpa. "Yes, ridiculous child . . . oh, you ridiculous child . . . stop that, you ri-dic-u-louse CHILD!" They ran toward Grandpa, shouting, then as he shook his fist at them, they pretended to dash away in fright. He caught one of the boys, Eddy Tanner, and gripped him by the shoulder.

"You fresh little punk," he said, "you want me to shake some sense into you." His voice was high.

Eddy, a skinny boy in a pink shirt, looked scared. "Let go of me. What do you think you're doing!"

Gail's face had turned a furious red. "Grandpa, stop that! Let Eddy go."

"Let Eddy go," someone else echoed. "Free Eddy Tanner." A mad hilarity seemed to take hold of the group. "Free Eddy Tanner, free Eddy Tanner," they yelled, laughing and surging toward Grandpa.

Frightened by the pinched look around Grandpa's mouth and the way his hand was dug into Eddy's shoulder, Jenny ran to the old man. "Grandpa, stop. Let's go in and play cards again. Grandpa, come on!"

"Ow, man, you're hurting me," Eddy howled. "Let go of me. Let go, you old fart!"

Just then three boys charged toward Grandpa, knocking into him. The force of their combined weight shook his hand from Eddy's shoulder and slammed him against the wall. "We freed Eddy," they yelled. Then, laughing hysterically, most of the party spilled up the concrete steps leading to the backyard.

"Are you all right, Grandpa?" Jenny said. "Are you okay? Did they hurt you?"

Breathing heavily, flushed and sweating, Grandpa remained leaning against the wall. He waved his hand slowly back and forth to indicate he was all right, but he seemed stunned. The cellar was nearly empty. Voices shouted down the street. Gail looked around, then turned on Grandpa. "You ruined my party!" Her voice was choked with tears. "It's all your fault, all your fault, Grandpa!"

"You shut up," Jenny said. "Just shut up!"

# Chapter 10

Sunday morning at breakfast, Gail complained bitterly to her parents about Grandpa's ruining her party. "It wasn't his fault," Jenny broke in. "I told you to turn down the noise. You wouldn't listen."

"Noise! It was music. I think I ought to be able to have a party in my own home once in a while. Mom, do you think that's wrong?" Gail's eyes filled with tears and the lids reddened. "It was so humiliating. Grandpa roaring around like a crazy man, scaring everyone, and practically wrecking the phonograph—"

"He did not!"

"Jenny, be quiet. Let Gail finish her story."

"Story is right. What about her hoody friends—"

"Jenny!"

"And then he caught Eddy Tanner and shook him like a dog. I mean, he acted crazy! Like a little music drove him crazy."

"It's really too bad the way things turned out," Valerie said. "Too bad Gail's party was wrecked, too bad Grandpa got upset." And she added that if she and Vince had been living in the basement apartment, nothing like this would ever have happened. They wouldn't have minded the noise and spirited activities of Gail's friends because they were, themselves, part of the young generation.

You sound like a soft-drink ad, Jenny thought. She poked at the yolk of her soft-boiled egg.

"Maybe there was a lot of noise," Mr. Pennoyer said. "I know how kids can get, but Pop overreacted."

"That's putting it mildly," Gail sniffed. "He acted like an old madman!"

"I can't eat this egg," Jenny said, pushing away her saucer. "It's making me nauseous."

"It's a perfectly good egg," her mother said, pushing the saucer back toward her. "Do you know what fresh eggs cost?"

"I'm not hungry."

"Eat your egg," her father said. "Your mother's got enough on her head without arguing with you."

Jenny poked the spoon into the yolk. Slimy. She touched the tip of her tongue to the spoon and shuddered.

"It seems like there's not a moment of peace around here anymore," her mother said. "Why is Grandpa so stubborn?"

"Maybe he's stubborn, but I can out-stubborn him," her father said. "We're not going on this way indefinitely, I can tell you that right now."

Jenny let another slimy drip of egg slither down her throat. She did feel nauseous. This whole conversation was making her nauseous. Didn't any of them understand how upset Grandpa had been last night? And whose fault was it that he was so jumpy and upset? Theirs, because they wouldn't leave him alone. It wasn't fair. No matter how she looked at it, the unfairness made her quiver with rage. Grandpa didn't bother anybody. He only wanted to be left alone to do the things he liked to do—take walks, play cards, read his old newspapers, and smoke his pipe. Sometimes he put little messages on the bulletin board just to remind them all that he still knew what was going on around him. But that was no crime. They weren't perfect, either.

After breakfast, when the dishes were done and Ethel had been taken for a walk outside in her stroller, Jenny went downstairs. "How are you, Grandpa?" she said, hugging him. "Are you feeling okay? Did you rest okay last night?"

He took his sweater off a hook on the wall and put it on. "It's chilly early this year," he said.

"No, Grandpa, it's a fantastic day outside," Jenny began. "I took Ethel for a walk, and it's really warm—" She stopped because he wasn't listening; he'd gone inward again. Jenny wanted to rush to him and hug him again and tell him not to worry, he was strong, and nobody could push him around. She tried to conjure up the picture of herself and Grandpa holding that lance across the door of his apartment, but remembering the stunned look in his eyes when those boys hurled him against the cellar wall, she found her imagination blocked.

"I'll do your dishes," she said, turning on the hot water tap.

"Eh?" Grandpa said. She'd never noticed before that he said "eh?" like an old man. She ran a glass under hot water. "Shall I put the kettle on for you, Grandpa? Did you eat breakfast this morning?"

"Don't fuss at me, child," he said. Someone tapped at the door. "Come in, come in!"

It was Mrs. Pennoyer, a yellow cardigan around her shoulders. "Grandpa, I—" Then, seeing Jenny, "You down here, Jenny? I told you to take Ethel out for a walk."

"I did," Jenny said quickly. "I walked her all the way up to Jericho Park, pushed her in the swings for a while, and then walked her back."

"Well, what are you doing now?"

"Just visiting Grandpa. Washing a few dishes for him." She tipped a cup into the drain.

"I wish you were so cooperative upstairs," Mrs. Pennoyer said. She sat down at the metal table. "Grandpa, the rent is due on your plot. I'm going to pay it from your social security check. All right?"

"Pay it or don't pay it. I don't want to hear about my own grave."

"Your grave," Jenny said. "What do you mean, your grave?"

"Ask your mother. This thing isn't my idea."

Mrs. Pennoyer brushed some crumbs off the table. "Your grandfather's being stubborn again. We bought him a beautiful burial plot, but every time we have to pay the rent, he makes a fuss."

"You bought him a *burial* plot," Jenny said. "Why?" Her voice went high, and her mother gave her a look. "Grandpa's living," Jenny said. "He doesn't need a burial plot."

"You are two of a kind," Mrs. Pennoyer said. "At least at your age it's understandable, but at your grandfather's age, it's plain undignified to act so thick. Facts are facts. Everybody needs a burial plot sooner or later. Maybe you don't realize how expensive that kind of thing can be, and how the prices are going up all the time. It's just good forward thinking to have a plot reserved and paid up beforehand."

"I think it's horrible," Jenny said.

"That's because you're a child. When your father and I get to that age, we'll do the same thing for ourselves, so as not to be a burden on our children when we go. The point is, we all have to go someday."

"Go?" Grandpa said blandly, tamping down his pipe with a thick thumb. "Go where?"

Mrs. Pennoyer's cheeks reddened. "Carl Pennoyer, you're trying to make a fool of me, and I resent it."

"Now, Amelia," Grandpa began.

"No, I mean it! Everyone passes away. My parents, God rest them, passed away. When people get to be senior citizens, their time is coming closer every day, and there's no use pretending it isn't so. All your little tricks can't change that. That's the way things are!"

Jenny put the last saucer in the drain and ran the cold water. Oh, stop it, she thought, please stop fighting with Grandpa. Slowly she drank a glass of cold water, feeling the ache of the cold all the way down to her stomach.

Later that night, it was Mr. Pennoyer who noticed the brown paper bag pinned to the kitchen bulletin board. On it in Grandpa's unmistakable wobbly hand-writing was a penciled message:

"I ain't going to 'pass away.' I'm going to die.

"My time ain't going 'to come.' I'll be dead.

"I ain't a 'senior citizen.' I'm an old codger of eighty-three."

"For Christ's sake," Mr. Pennoyer breathed, tearing down the bag and crumpling it. "What's the matter with Pop? What is this, a war?"

# Chapter 11

"Valerie worked all afternoon on this," Mrs. Pennoyer said, setting the large serving bowl filled with food in the middle of the table. "Frankie, you start it around."

Frankie dipped several spoonfuls of the mixture onto his plate and passed the bowl to Vince. "What is it?" he said, sprinkling salt over the food without tasting it.

"It's called Spicy Steak Bits," Valerie said. "It's a Malaysian recipe from my *Eating-Round-the-World* cookbook. Here, take rice, Frankie, it's supposed to be eaten with rice."

"Terrific, honey," Vince said, making an ecstatic face. "Really great!"

Grandpa passed the bowl of Spicy Steak Bits without taking any. "All I'd like is a well-done hamburger, Amelia," he said.

"A hamburger?" Jenny's mother said. "Valerie went to a lot of trouble to make this meal. And it's very nutritious."

"I wish you'd taste it, Grandpa Pennoyer," Valerie said, "give it a chance. There are only good things in it."

"I never had a taste for spicy food," he said.

"I've found that old people can be very narrow-minded," Valerie said. "They get into a rut and are afraid to try anything new, even when it's good for them."

"I think this is yum yum delicious," Gail said. "Try it, Grandpa, you'll like it."

"I'm sure it's fine," Grandpa said, pushing away the bowl. "If I could have a hamburger, Amelia—"

"I can't cater to everyone's individual tastes," Mrs. Pennoyer said. "This is a home, not a restaurant. I'm sorry, Grandpa, but if you don't care for what's on the table tonight, you'll just have to go without."

"I'll make Grandpa a hamburger." Jenny started to rise.

"Sit down," her father said. "Stay where you are."

"I was just going to help Grandpa—"

"I know what you were going to do, and I'm telling you to sit down and shut up. For a change, I'd like to have one peaceful meal around here."

Jenny sat down and shut up, but she found it difficult to eat. Grandpa had left the table and gone downstairs. He could do that, but she had to sit there and pretend to love Valerie's food and try not to look too mad, because her father was really on the warpath. When he got that way, stabbing into his meat and tearing apart the bread, he was capable of taking away her privileges for a month for nothing more than a cross-eyed look. She stuffed in another bite of the gluey mix and chewed hard.

The next few nights Grandpa didn't show up for supper. "How long is that man going to keep this up?" Mrs. Pennoyer said.

"He's making his own meals," Jenny said.

"Why is he doing that? There's more than enough up here."

"You know Pop. Got his back up the other night, and now he's letting us know."

"Well, I don't know what to think," Mrs. Pennoyer said. "I'm certainly willing for him to eat with us."

"Don't blame yourself," Mr. Pennoyer said. "Nothing to blame yourself for."

Thursday night Jenny went downstairs after supper. Grandpa was standing at his little stove, frying a piece of meat. On the table he'd set out a glass of tea and a plate of crackers. "Is that all you're having for supper?" Jenny said.

"Plenty, plenty," Grandpa said. "I should have done this a long time ago. Your father always did eat too early for me."

"I wish you'd change your mind," Jenny said. "It doesn't feel right eating without you at the table."

"Eh?" he said. "One less person, that's all. Let's talk about something else." He picked up one of his old newspapers. "Now listen to this, Jenny, here's a father and son who were reunited after being separated for forty years. Now what do you think of that? Forty years."

Outside, a wind had sprung up and was rattling around the house. Hard drops of rain pelted against the windows. "Rain again," Jenny said. "It's rained nearly every day this fall so far." Grandpa put the newspaper down on the shelf next to the stove and turned to check a window fastening. As he did—Jenny saw it happen so fast she couldn't do more than cry out—grease from the meat splattered out of the pan and onto the gas flame, which flared up and caught the dry newspaper. In an instant, flames were licking at the grimy wall behind the stove and climbing rapidly toward the ceiling. "Grandpa!" Jenny cried. The old man turned, and his face went pale as clay.

"A blanket," he said hoarsely. "Quick, Jenny, a blanket."

Jenny ran into his bedroom and snatched the gray wool blanket from his bed. Grandpa took it and began beating at the flames. Jenny threw a glass of water at the wall, then ran to the door, flung it open, and yelled, "Fire! Fire, fire!"

Within moments, most of the Pennoyer family was downstairs. The fire was out by then, but Frankie, armed with the fire extinguisher that had hung for years behind the cellar door, squirted happily away, throwing a cloud of white chemical foam over the kitchen walls, the stove, and the sink.

Mr. Pennoyer opened windows and ordered everyone out. "I'll stay," Grandpa said thinly. His eyes were red, and he was coughing. "It was just a grease fire." He waved his arms at the smoke.

"Pop, we're all going upstairs. You, too."

Mrs. Pennoyer took Grandpa's arm. "This smoke is no good for you. It'll irritate your lungs."

"I have to clean up," Grandpa said, trying to free his arm. His voice shook.

"I'll help clean up," Jenny said.

"Nobody's cleaning anything now," Mr. Pennoyer said. "It's too damn smoky to even stay down here. Pop, stop being so stubborn. You come upstairs with us. Everyone upstairs," he ordered. "All out." He took Grandpa's other arm and between them, he and Mrs. Pennoyer easily steered the old man to the door and up the cellar stairs.

"Grandpa's still trembling," Mrs. Pennoyer said as they mounted the cellar steps. "Poor old Grandpa. Thank goodness nothing worse happened. I'm so afraid of fire. It's one of my worst nightmares that this house will catch fire. How could you have been so careless, Grandpa?"

"It could have happened to anyone," Jenny said.

"Oh, really?" Mrs. Pennoyer said. "Well, it's never happened before."

In the kitchen Mrs. Pennoyer insisted that Grandpa drink a cup of hot milk. "You're shaking," she said. Then to Mr. Pennoyer, "Frank, Grandpa can sleep on the couch tonight, and we'll take out the folding cot for Frankie. It's not very comfortable, but one night won't hurt him."

"No, no, don't bother, I'm going downstairs in a little while," Grandpa said querulously. He put down his cup and the hot milk sloshed over onto the table.

"You're staying up here, Pop," Mr. Pennoyer said, "you're not up to taking care of yourself tonight. Jenny, wipe up this mess here where Grandpa spilled. Pop, quit fighting, will you?"

When Jenny came home from school the next day, Grandpa and Vince were both downstairs. Vince, on a ladder, was scrubbing the walls with a stiff, soapy brush, while Grandpa, broom in hand, made fitful stabs at the floor. The windows were open and the furniture pushed into the middle of the room to allow Vince to get at the walls. The smell of smoke was everywhere.

"I told you not to try working, Grandpa," Vince said, coming off the ladder. "Here, don't tire yourself." He took the broom from Grandpa. "Go upstairs with Jenny and leave the cleanup to me. Just leave it all to me."

Grandpa slept on the couch again that night while Frankie, grumbling about his rear end freezing, slept on the folding cot. The following night he moved back to his own room, taking the top bunk so Grandpa could have the bottom bunk, and Vince and Valerie went downstairs to the apartment to "rough it" (as Valerie said) until the apartment had been completely repainted and made livable again. The painting and cleaning went on all week.

"When are they going to be finished fussing?" Grandpa asked, and at first went up and down the stairs to his apartment several times a day. But there was nothing for him to do and mostly he hung around the house chewing aspirin and getting in Mrs. Pennoyer's way. He seemed to get more and more tired as the days went on and developed a heavy cough. Finally he lost his voice, was coughing up a thick mucousy phlegm, and took to his bed, submitting to Mrs. Pennoyer's diet of fruit juice, thin cereal, and no tobacco.

Jenny hung around Frankie's bedroom, but Grandpa was too sick to be interested in anything. He became so weak and wobbly that Mrs. Pennoyer insisted on leading him to the bathroom. Day and night he wore one or the other of the two long blue and white striped nightshirts that she had bought for him, beneath which his legs looked white and frail. "Now don't lock the door," Mrs. Pennoyer said when she left him in the bathroom. "Just call if you need me for anything."

"Let go, I'll be all right," he whispered hoarsely, prying at her fingers. "Go on out."

"You're not all right," Mrs. Pennoyer said soothingly. "You're weak and sick, dear."

# Chapter 12

Grandpa was sick for ten days, and all that time the smell of fresh paint and the sounds of hammering drifted through the house. Vince and Valerie worked on the apartment in every spare moment. "It's coming along," Vince said. "It's going to be something when we're done. Valerie's a perfectionist—has to have everything just so."

Since the fire Jenny had hardly been downstairs. She was reluctant to see Grandpa's apartment changed. But changed wasn't the word. The night she finally decided to go down there she saw that it had been transformed. Everything was brighter and cleaner. Grandpa's furniture was out of sight in the middle of the room under a paint-spattered plastic drop cloth. The floors had been stripped of the old scabby-looking linoleum; the walls were freshly painted cream with a sizzling blue on the woodwork. The cubicle for the toilet had been painted sunflower yellow, and there was a new bright yellow toilet seat. In the bedroom Valerie was painting the window frame blue. The window itself was different—it had been enlarged and new double glass set in. Jenny looked and looked, as if by looking long enough she would finally see Grandpa's familiar apartment again.

"Hi, there, that you, Jenny?" Valerie called. "Come to help the painting brigade?"

"No," Jenny said. "I'm looking for something of Grandpa's." She burrowed under the plastic drop cloth and found the deck of cards in the sideboard drawer.

"Hey, Jen," her brother said, "come on over here and see how things are progressing." He was wearing a carpenter's apron and, screwdriver in hand, was putting up new birchwood cabinets in the kitchen. Jenny looked at the brand-new glistening stainless steel sink, and the brick design asphalt floor tiles piled in a corner. "How do you like it?" her brother said. He took a silver-wrapped chocolate from his pocket and held it out to her. "Looks great, doesn't it?"

"Vince—all this fixing up, you're doing it for Grandpa, aren't you?"

"For Grandpa?" Vince repeated.

"Yes. For when he gets better and wants to come back to his own home. Oh, I think it's nice of you and Valerie to—"

"Hey, Jenny, wait, wait." A queer look had come over Vince's face, as if his features had somehow slipped sideways.

"Listen, Jen—" He came down the ladder and put his arm around her. "Try to understand our side of it, honey. Val and I need a place of our own. We're just starting out, but Grandpa, he's finished. No, wait, I don't mean it that way. What I mean is, he doesn't need it as much as we do. He can't take care of himself alone anymore. You know what I mean. He's a sick old guy. Listen, Jen, I have feelings about him, just as much as you—"

"I know what you mean," Jenny said, flinging off his arm. "I know what you mean, you creep!" The candy she'd swallowed stuck like a lump in her stomach as she ran out, slamming the door.

She found her mother sorting through Grandpa's clothes the next day. "Hello, Jenny, come to help?" Mrs. Pennoyer said, strangely echoing what Valerie had said the night before.

Jenny shook her head. "No—I just—" She didn't finish. She didn't know why she'd come downstairs. She felt miserable and unhappy. Her mother held up Grandpa's black coat. "This old thing," she said, "look

at it. It's incredible." The pockets, collar, and cuffs
were frayed to a fare-thee-well, and every button was
mismatched and hanging by a thread. Mrs. Pennoyer
had already filled several cardboard boxes with an accumulation of clothes and other things from Grandpa's cupboards, bureau drawers, and closet. "I'll buy
him a new coat with a fur collar and decent warm
cuffs," she said, throwing the shapeless black coat into
a half-filled carton. "This can go, too." She added
Grandpa's brown wool sweater with the sagging
pockets.

"That's Grandpa's favorite sweater," Jenny said.

"I'll buy him a better one. This one actually smells."

Did Grandpa know what they were doing? Did he
care? Jenny went slowly upstairs and into Frankie's
room. Grandpa was lying on his back on the bottom
bunk, covered with a mound of blankets, eyes closed,
hands twitching. There was a tray on the floor with
a half emptied bowl of soup and a glass that had held
fruit juice. "Grandpa," Jenny said. "Grandpa, how
do you feel?" His eyelids fluttered, but he didn't say
anything. "Grandpa, you're awake. Do you feel any
better?"

"No."

"Does your chest still hurt?"

He nodded. Jenny sat down by his side and touched
the back of his hand. Why didn't he sit up? Why
didn't he do something? She wanted to hug him
and then she wanted to shake him. "Grandpa, do you
want me to write a note for you?"

A spasm of coughing shook him. His eyes watered.
"Note?" he said harshly.

"You know! To put on the bulletin board. Don't
you want to say anything? Tell them some things?"

His hands plucked at the blanket cover. "I have to
sleep. Go away."

That night Jenny dreamed that she was running
down a dark, shiny street, shiny as patent leather.
Grandpa was running with her, holding her hand.

People on yellow bicycles were honking at them and screaming with laughter. Run, Grandpa, she wanted to scream, run, run, hurry! Hurry! HURRY!

Jenny woke, her heart pounding fearfully. Everything in the house was quiet and dark. She heard the baby stirring in her crib and sucking her lips. The floor creaked. Outside, a car raced past. Leaves were falling on the roof and on the sidewalk with a papery whispering sound. There was a tight band around Jenny's chest. She wanted to get out of bed, tiptoe into Frankie's room, shake Grandpa's bony shoulder, and say urgently, "Grandpa, wake up! You must wake up!" Oh, how crazy. Nobody did a thing like that in the middle of the night—and to a sick man. She didn't move, and in a few moments she fell asleep again.

In the morning, still dazed with sleep, feeling troubled and depressed, she was sent downstairs to fetch Valerie. "Jenny, quickly now! It's a long distance phone call," Mrs. Pennoyer said, covering the mouthpiece of the phone with her hand. Vince and Valerie were eating breakfast, sitting at the table under the window. "There's a phone call for you," Jenny said. The sight of them so at home there produced a lump in her throat.

"For me?" Vince pushed back his chair.

"No. For Valerie. Long distance."

"Long distance!" Valerie jumped up. She was barefooted, wearing one of Vince's shirts over a pair of tights, and had her hair in one long braid. "Vince, it must be my mother!"

Trailing them up the stairs, Jenny imagined Valerie's mother on the other end of the wire, saying, *Come home, Valerie dear, we miss you . . . we want you to live with us, you and Vince . . . we have plenty of room for you, and lots of money to give you . . .*

Upstairs, Vince stood next to Valerie, his arm around her shoulder while she spoke on the phone. "Mom!" she said. "Oh, Mom . . ." She listened for a long time, nodding, and sometimes saying, "Yes, I see . . . Yes I understand . . . yes . . . yes . . . yes, I do, no I mean it . . ."

Sitting at the table, Jenny mentally packed their duffels and cases. She threw in the bottles, the books, and the stuffed cats. She found out about plane schedules. She was at the airport, waving goodbye to them. So long, Vince and Valerie! Toodle-oo and bon voyage!

Hanging up the phone, Valerie wiped her eyes with the tail of Vince's shirt. "Isn't that silly, crying?" she said. "But I couldn't help it, hearing Mom's voice."

"Is everything all right now?" Mrs. Pennoyer said.

"Well, it's better, anyway," Valerie said. "They're still not exactly thrilled about my being married, but I guess they're starting to accept it."

"They want you back, don't they?" Jenny said. "Are you going soon?" *Vince and Valerie are gone. Grandpa is downstairs in his own apartment again. Jenny is knocking on the door in the morning. "Who is it?" Grandpa says grumpily. "It's me, Grandpa." Jenny comes in, he's sitting by the window, she kisses his cheek . . .*

"I knew your folks would come through," Vince said.

"They must miss you a lot," Jenny said. "I bet they really want to see you and Vince. When are you leaving?"

Valerie reached for a piece of dry toast and nibbled it. "Leave for where? My father's company is sending him to France for a year. They're all going over, and my sister Felicia is going to school there."

"France," Mrs. Pennoyer said. "How exciting."

"Then nobody's going to be in your home," Jenny said. So long!

"Oh, sure there is," Valerie said. "My parents have subleased their apartment for the year."

Jenny slumped down in her chair. What was the matter with her? Didn't she know by now that Vince and Valerie had no intention of leaving, and that Grandpa wasn't going to get back his apartment? Not now, not next week, not next month, not ever.

Later that day, the junkman parked his battered pick-up truck in the Pennoyer driveway and hauled away Grandpa's thirteen-year accumulation of newspapers. On the junkman's heels a big red Salvation Army truck backed up to the cellar door and three men began carrying Grandpa's possessions up the back cellar steps and loading them into the truck: the iron bedstead, the heavy old sideboard, the metal kitchen table with the enameled top, four wooden chairs, the bureau and mirror that had stood at the foot of the bed in the tiny bedroom, the old square mahogany victrola with the scratchy head and even the box of 78 rpm records.

Everything is going, Jenny thought, watching the men, and for a moment she felt as dizzy as if she were falling through space.

All that remained was the old Boston rocker with its flattened rockers that Mrs. Pennoyer put in Frankie's room, saying she thought Grandpa would like something of his own there. The men from the Salvation Army truck were also going to take away the tiny refrigerator, but at the last moment Valerie pointed out that it could be kept in the cellar filled with soft drinks for future parties.

Two men climbed into the cab of the truck. The third swung the heavy back doors shut and began fastening a chain. "Wait. Could you open it again?" Jenny asked. "Please?" she added as the man looked annoyed. The cardboard boxes had been loaded in last. "There—that one," she said. "Could you push it over to me? I want something." She snatched out Grandpa's old black coat and held it against her chest.

The man laughed. "Is that the new style?"

# Chapter 13

One night, having crept out of bed to use the bathroom, Jenny saw a light on in the kitchen and found
Grandpa there, wrapped in a blanket, drinking tea. It
was two in the morning. "Jenny," he said. She sat
down with him. His health was improving. He now
resisted her mother's efforts to keep him in bed or in
the Boston rocker all day. Instead he shuffled slowly
around the house, holding onto walls and furniture.
At supper the night before last, Mrs. Pennoyer had
said that she had never felt as tied down: she didn't
dare step out of the house even for five minutes because she worried so about Grandpa. What if something should happen to him? What if he started another fire? She'd never forgive herself, she said.

"Have some tea," Grandpa said to Jenny. He
poured hot water from the kettle into a cup, spilling
a little. His mouth moved soundlessly.

Jenny put a napkin on the spill and watched the
paper blot up the water. "Can't you sleep, Grandpa?"
She dunked her tea bag up and down, then heaped in
the sugar.

"Just restless," he sighed.

Jenny put her hand over his. "Grandpa—" What
could she say to bring him comfort? They'd taken
away his home, and she couldn't give it back to him.

The next night Grandpa was afoot again. Mr. Pennoyer, lying in bed, heard someone move stealthily
around the house and thought it was an intruder.
"Who's there?" he called, and leaping out of bed he

banged into a chair, swore at the top of his voice, and woke most of the family. When he found out that the "intruder" was Grandpa, who looked astonished at all the noise, Mr. Pennoyer was furious. In the morning he was tired and irritable.

"You prowl around like that often, Pop?" he said, rattling the morning paper.

"Nights I can't sleep, yes, I get up, walk around, try not to disturb anybody," Grandpa said. He was slowly chewing a piece of dry toast.

"I don't want you to do that anymore," Mr. Pennoyer said. "If you can't sleep at night you can sleep all day, but other people aren't so lucky. Other people have to go to work and need their rest. You get the message, Pop? You stay in bed at night where you belong."

"Well, I get restless, and my bones ache—can't sleep so good—"

"Count sheep," Gail said.

"I'm going to make sure you get a glass of hot milk before bedtime," Mrs. Pennoyer said. "It'll make you drowsy."

"I don't see anything so terrible about Grandpa getting up sometimes in the night," Jenny said.

"The radio," Mr. Pennoyer said, snapping his fingers. "That'll do the trick for you, Pop." The radio was Mr. Pennoyer's own transistor set with a plastic earplug. "Instead of getting out of bed when you can't sleep, Pop, lie still and listen to the radio. I do it when I've got something on my mind, and it has a nice soothing effect. So long as you keep that earplug in, no one will even know you've got the thing turned on."

Either Grandpa didn't walk the next night or he did it so quietly that nobody knew. Mr. Pennoyer was sure the radio was working its soothing spell. "It works, doesn't it, Pop?" he said. Grandpa grunted something that might have been yes or might have been no.

A few nights later when Grandpa couldn't sleep and was attempting to oblige his son by listening to the radio, the earplug jack unfortunately pulled out of its socket (perhaps Grandpa hadn't put it in securely enough), and voices suddenly blared through the sleeping house. In the darkness Grandpa fumbled with the knobs, but because his hands were so stiff and clumsy he only succeeded in knocking the set off the bed so that it crashed to the floor with the frantic voice of the disc jockey announcing the next selection, "FOR MARCIA AND TIM, HEDDA AND VICK, AND RIMA THE BIRD GIRL . . ."

Jenny came bolt awake at the frantically gay voice sawing through her dreams, Ethel began crying, and Gail sat up in bed, saying, "What is it this time? Is it that old madman again?"

Jenny shoved her feet into her slippers and ran for Frankie's room. By then lights were turning on all over the house. "Sorry, Frank," Grandpa was saying to Jenny's father, who was clutching his pajama bottoms. "My hands, you know, they're stiff at night—"

"All right, all right," her father said. "There's always some reason, isn't there? Go on back to bed, everybody." He waved his arms. "Go on, Jenny!"

"In a minute, Dad." She went to her grandfather and bent over the bottom bunk. "Are you okay, Grandpa?" He lay back, closing his eyes, and nodded.

"Jenny! Come on," her father said. "I want to get back to sleep." He snapped the light off and on, then off again.

That Sunday Jenny and Grandpa found themselves alone in the house, and Jenny was delighted. Mr. and Mrs. Pennoyer had gone for a ride with Ethel and Gail. Vince and Valerie were visiting friends, and despite the rain Frankie was out running. There was no one to complain about Grandpa doing this or Grandpa not doing that. Jenny was sick of hearing the family grievances about Grandpa. She could recite them all, backward, forward, and inside out.

She got out their deck of cards, made a pot of tea for Grandpa, and opened a bottle of soda for herself. Outside, cars sloshed by, headlights on to penetrate the gloomy rain. Sitting at the table across from Grandpa, Jenny thought it was almost like so many other afternoons they'd spent together—the standing lamp casting a sheen over the bare dark wood of the table, rain smearing the windowpanes, and the cards flick, flick, flicking in the silence.

"Ha, ha! Gin!" Grandpa rubbed his hands together. He was dressed today, wearing baggy trousers, an undershirt, and the new cardigan Mrs. Pennoyer had bought him. The sweater seemed to irritate him and he twisted his shoulders uncomfortably every few minutes.

A door banged below, then busy sounds came up from the apartment. Vince and Valerie were back. Jenny glanced at Grandpa. They never mentioned his old apartment or Vince and Valerie being there. Grandpa's face was blank, too blank. She knew he had heard them.

"Let's play another hand," she said. "I'll be reckless. Penny a point."

"Profligate with your money, my girl. All right. Watch yourself now. I'm out for blood."

Time passed so pleasantly that Jenny was surprised when she heard the front door swing open. Mrs. Pennoyer came in, took off her scarf, and shook raindrops off her coat. "You two still at it? Better clear the table, Jenny, it's nearly suppertime. Grandpa, you want to eat with us tonight? I've got a roast in the oven."

"Tray'll be fine," he said.

"Still being stubborn, old dear?" said Mrs. Pennoyer, obviously in good humor, as she pinched his cheek. "Well, do as you will, it's not my throat you're cutting."

Gail came in then, carrying Ethel, and after her their father, toting a brown paper grocery bag. "Hot rolls, hot rolls for supper," he called. His thinning hair had been plastered to his head by the rain. Ethel toddled to Jenny, who swung her into the air. Gail, looking at herself in the mirror over the buffet, said, "Guess where we went?"

"Give me a hint," Jenny said.

"Gail," Mrs. Pennoyer called warningly from the kitchen, "remember what I told you."

"Well, where'd you go?" Jenny said.

"Never mind." She tried to take Grandpa's arm. "Want me to help you to your room?" Her tone was as sweet as if she'd never called him "an old madman."

"No need." Grandpa shuffled slowly off toward Frankie's room, moving his shoulders irritably under the new sweater. Jenny put Ethel down and wrapped a rubber band around the deck of cards. She took Grandpa's cup and the empty soda bottle into the kitchen. "Where'd you go, Mom?" she said as she rinsed the teacup and dropped the soda bottle into the garbage can.

"For a ride," Mrs. Pennoyer said, taking salad makings from the refrigerator.

"Where?" Jenny said.

Mrs. Pennoyer filled a pan with water and set it on the stove. "We just rode around," she said vaguely. "Looked at new houses and other things."

"Well, what did you see?" Jenny persisted.

"Oh, not much. The rain and all, you know. But it was nice getting out." She wasn't going to say where they'd been, what they'd done, what Gail's "Guess where we went" meant. "Set the table, Jenny. Gail! Gail, come here. Go ask Vince and Valerie if they want to share the roast tonight."

In a little while Vince and Valerie came up, their arms around each other. Valerie picked up Ethel and kissed her neck. "You're the sweetest. Hope I have a sweetie like you someday."

"You will, you will, sure as time and the tide," Mr. Pennoyer said. "Just make sure it isn't too soon."

"Now Dad," Valerie said, smiling, "don't get personal."

"Vince—beer?" Mr. Pennoyer asked, going into the refrigerator.

Frankie ambled in then and said he'd like a beer, too, and Mr. Pennoyer said no, positively not, Frankie wasn't going to get a beer or any other drink until he was eighteen. "And don't forget it," he added.

Vince winked at Frankie. "I got the same lecture at your age, kid, and look at me now."

"I heard the Burleys down the street bought a brand-new thirty-five cubic foot double-door freezer," Mrs. Pennoyer said, testing the roast with a fork. "We could use a freezer, Frank. It could easily go in the cellar."

"I was thinking of buying a TV for our bedroom," Mr. Pennoyer said. "Can't do both right now."

"Yah, Daddy," Gail said. "Two TVs! Did I tell you, Mom, that Sylvia Forrester at school has her own TV and her own telephone in her bedroom."

The talk flowed on, amiable, relaxed. Valerie and Gail set the table. Jenny transferred the margarine from its foil wrapping to a glass-covered dish. Mr. Pennoyer asked Vince to sharpen the carving knife, and Frankie was rapped on the hand for snitching a hot roll before they sat down. Jenny kept quiet and listened. In her mind, she was hearing Gail saying, *Guess where we went . . . guess where we went . . . guess where we went . . .* Something had happened this afternoon on that ride; while Jenny and Grandpa were sitting home, playing cards, something had changed. Jenny could sense it, feel it, nearly smell it, and she was sure it had to do with Grandpa.

It was Gail's turn to help with the dishes that night. Jenny bathed Ethel, then read her a story, covered her, put out the light, and closed the door. "Ja, Ja!" Ethel called.

Jenny opened the door a crack. "What is it, honey?"

"Stay!" It was Ethel's new word, uttered in a firm, commanding voice.

"I'll stay right outside your door until you fall asleep," Jenny promised. She closed the door again.

"Ja, Ja!"

"I'm here. Go to sleep," Jenny said, leaning against the wall. Gail came out of the bathroom. "Have a good ride this afternoon?" Jenny said. "Have fun?"

Gail pushed up the sleeves of her sweater. "Am I getting a pimple right here on my chin?"

"Did Dad buy you ice cream?"

"Sure." Gail fingered her chin. "He always does. I had Hawaiian Pineapple."

"Where exactly did you go?"

"We—" Gail put her hand to her mouth. "We just drove around."

"You were going to say something else."

"I know I shouldn't squeeze this," Gail said, pressing the red lump. "How does it look to you?"

"Gail! Where'd you go? The pimple looks like a pimple. Leave it alone and tell me where you went."

"Mom told me not to say anything. You heard her."

"I want to know where you went, Gail Pennoyer."

"Ask Mom," Gail said. "I'm going to go look at this pimple. Maybe I should squeeze it."

Jenny caught her sister's arm. "Tell me where you went," she said, putting into her voice and her eyes all her caring, all of her need to know what they had been doing, and how it concerned Grandpa. "*Tell me.*"

"We drove around," Gail said after a moment.

"I know that. What else?"

"Let go of me. You're pulling my sweater all out of shape."

"You tell me and I'll let go."

"You let go and I'll tell you."

Jenny dropped her hand. "Now tell!"

"We drove around and we looked at those new

houses they're building over in Vernon Acres and we had ice cream, and then . . ." Gail shrugged. "We stopped up on Snooks Hill where they have . . . where there's this place, a home for old people called Castle Haven."

"Go on," Jenny said.

Gail worried her chin. "That's all. We stopped and looked at this place, this Castle Haven, and Mom and Dad talked about it and said it looked like a real nice place for Grandpa. Real clean and neat and nice. And they said they'd go see it, maybe next weekend, and talk to the lady who runs it."

"If you're lying to me, Gail Pennoyer—"

"I'm not lying! I don't lie. They talked about it. They said Grandpa is failing and he needs professional care—"

"Failing," Jenny said. She was burning with rage and fear. "Failing what? I didn't know he had to take a test."

"You know what I mean. He's getting to be too much for Mom with everything else she has to do. He isn't the way he used to be, like he mumbles to himself all the time, and the way he wakes everybody up at night. And I heard Mom say that when he uses the bathroom he's careless. He misses the bowl."

"Oh, shut up," Jenny said inadequately. "Just shut up!" Misery had her by the throat. She walked away from Gail and locked herself in the bathroom where she sat on the toilet and, bent over, clutching her middle, thought about Grandpa and her parents and this place—this home, this castle for old people. Castle—oh, that was good, very good. Really excellent, she thought bitterly. As good as her mother's calling Grandpa's grave his "resting place." Pretty words for ugly things! Grandpa hated those cover-up words, those figures of speech, and now so did she! Everything was a figure of speech to her parents—everything they didn't want to think about—even Grandpa himself!

# *Chapter 14*

"Jenny Pennoyer."

"Hi, Rhoda," Jenny said in a muted voice.

"Well, goldang!" Rhoda was trying, so Jenny pushed out a smile.

"Elephant joke," Rhoda said. "What did the elephant say when the VW ran into it?"

"Rhoda—"

"How many times have I told you kiddies, no playing in the road!"

"Ha, ha," Jenny said quietly.

Rhoda looked at her, pushed her hands through the short frizzy bush of hair. "Hey, you can laugh better than that. What do you need, another elephant joke?"

"Rhoda, don't."

"Girl, what's the trouble. You sound like you lost your best friend, but that can't be possible, because here I am."

"Rhoda, listen. My parents went for a ride yesterday and they . . . they . . ." She clenched her lips. She didn't want to say the words.

"Hey, Jenny, what is it? What happened?"

A group of boys rushed past them. "Rhoda Rivers," one of them yelled, "go on home, your momma's calling you." They all laughed.

Jenny waited until the boys were far past them. "Rhoda, my parents went to see an old people's home. For Grandpa."

"A place for your grandfather to go, to live there?"

"Yes."

Rhoda sidestepped a pile of dog droppings. "Is it a nice one?"

"How do I know? What do I care!"

"Well, it matters, Jenny. I mean, some of those places are awful, but some of them are nifty. I bet your parents picked a nice one."

"A nice one. A nice one! Are you stupid or something?"

"Well, look at it this way—don't be so upset, maybe your grandfather will really like it. Maybe—"

"Are you crazy?" Jenny felt that in a moment she would either scream or break into tears.

"You don't know, Jenny. He'll be with people like himself—"

"I don't want to talk about it!" Jenny pushed past Rhoda and began walking very fast up the hill. There was a sick, sour taste in the back of her throat.

At home, no one said anything about an old people's home and, therefore, Jenny didn't ask. What wasn't mentioned might not be true. Forget it, push it aside, bury the worry and fear, go on as usual.

Monday passed, Tuesday, then Wednesday. Still, nobody mentioned "homes" or "castles." Thursday after school she took Ethel out in the stroller and Grandpa came along for the walk. He looked better and was walking with a cane, complaining about not having his tobacco. "Been smoking my pipe for sixty-five years. Damn fool idea to try and make me give it up now. Trying to teach an old dog new tricks."

"It's better for you, Grandpa," Jenny said. She picked up a bright scarlet maple leaf and handed it to Ethel. "Say leaf, honey. Leaf."

"Wah, wah," Ethel said, pointing to a puddle. She hit her hands on the stroller tray. "Wah! Wah!"

"She's hopeless," Jenny said to Grandpa.

Friday evening he sat with the family in the living room and watched TV. On the screen, a comedienne wearing a long, shapeless black dress and a little pie-shaped hat sat down on a park bench. Her mouth folded into a tiny prim square, she fussed anxiously with her big flat pocketbook and looked suspiciously around her. An old man with a drooping mustache, leaning heavily on a cane, approached.

"Did I ever tell you about the time I hitchhiked all over the country, Jenny?" Grandpa said.

"Shhh!" Gail flapped her hands impatiently and leaned toward the screen.

"You were fifteen, weren't you?" Jenny said.

Grandpa nodded. "A boy of fifteen. I hitched through twenty states, on my own for nearly a year before I got home—"

"Grandpa, please!"

"Pop, will you pipe down, this is a good show."

Jenny touched his hand. On the screen the old man had sat down next to the woman. She was giving him suspicious glances. With every little suspicious glare, the audience roared.

"Nice day," the old man squeaked timidly.

"What!" the woman cried in outrage. "What did you say?"

"Nice day," he said even more timidly.

"I thought so," she cried, and raising her big pocketbook she hit him over the head, knocked him about the shoulders, and finally toppled him over flat on his face on the ground. "That'll teach you," she said, stepping on his prone body and walking away.

"That kills me; that just kills me," Gail cried gleefully.


On Saturday afternoon Jenny took the bus downtown and looked for a birthday present for her mother. An umbrella? Writing paper? Sheet music? She couldn't find anything that satisfied her and went home empty-handed. Anyway, her mother's birthday was still two weeks away.

After supper there was TV again and buttered popcorn. Everything was ordinary, usual, and reassuring. Then on Sunday afternoon her parents said they were going for a drive. They were taking Ethel, did anyone else want to come? "Me," Gail said, trying on a scarf.

"You'll stay home with Grandpa, Jenny?" Mrs. Pennoyer asked, zipping Ethel into her sweater. "I don't want to leave him alone."

"Where are you going?" Jenny's palms felt damp. Were they going to that place again?

"Just going to drive around." Mrs. Pennoyer, holding Ethel around the middle, bent toward a mirror, smoothing a flake of powder off her nose.

"Come on. Let's go, whoever's going," Mr. Pennoyer called. "You stay home, Jenny."

If only she could unlock her tongue, come right out and ask, *Are you going to put Grandpa in that place? In a Home?* But what if they had forgotten, and her asking reminded them?

"I want to come with you," she said. She had to know for herself.

They all got into the car, parents in front, the three girls in the back seat. As her father was backing the car out of the driveway, Vince and Valerie came around the side of the house and waved. "I asked them to stay home," Mrs. Pennoyer said, "because of him."

*Him.* Say his name! Jenny thought. Grandpa! She stared out the window, biting her tongue, reminding herself that she couldn't afford to get in trouble with her father because she just had to go along on this ride.

"Caa," Ethel said, pointing to the traffic. "Caa."

"What a day," Mrs. Pennoyer said. "Aren't we lucky?" The air was bright and only a few puffy clouds floated in the sky. Mr. Pennoyer drove leisurely out of the city and up and down back roads where new houses were springing up like mushrooms after a rain. "Lavender shutters?" Mrs. Pennoyer said. "Now really."

"Did you see that barbecue pit, Amelia? I'd like to make one of those in our backyard."

"Can't burn in the city, Frank. There's an ordinance against it."

"Outdoor cooking is okay—oh, hey, look at that, swimming pool and all. That house must have cost fifty thou if it cost a penny—"

"Frank, I *like* that brickwork, don't you? And look at that gorgeous fencing they're putting up."

Jenny yawned. Her parents' voices melted in her head and made her feel sleepy. They often went on Sunday drives exactly like this, her father driving leisurely up and down different roads, her parents commenting on the expensive houses, the scenery blurring past her eyes. Today seemed no different, except for the awful thing Gail had told her. She sat up again, blinking and fearful. Where was Snooks Hill? Where was Castle Haven? Ethel, sucking on a piece of hard bread, crawled from Gail's lap to Jenny's and poked a soggy bit of bread from her mouth into Jenny's mouth. "Yuk," Jenny said, squeezing the baby.

They drove around for more than an hour and it was all the same. No Castle Haven. No old people's home. Jenny slid down in the seat. She had been so tense with expectation that now her back ached. Could Gail have been lying to her? She didn't know what to think, but began to let herself hope that it had all been a threat, a terrible moment of anger on her parents' part that was now dissipated. Relief made her feel giddy, and sorry, too, that she'd wasted a whole afternoon away from Grandpa. Oh, well, there would be more afternoons, Sunday after Sunday after Sunday to spend with him while her parents and Gail drove around looking at houses and fences and barbeque pits. She tickled Ethel, making a horrible face, crossing her eyes to amuse the baby, and making her laugh so hard that she hiccuped. "Ja, Ja!" she cried, smacking Jenny on the face.

Mrs. Pennoyer turned around. "Jenny, don't excite the baby so much."

"She loves it."

"Do you have to disagree with everything?" Mrs. Pennoyer said. And just then Mr. Pennoyer turned the car into a driveway and stopped. They were at the bottom of a graveled walk that led to a tall, green three-story house. There were a dozen empty green rockers on the wide front porch, and a maple tree with yellowish green leaves cast shade over the yard. There were a few empty metal chairs on the lawn, and a metal sign hanging from a metal post. "Castle Haven. Visiting Hours, 2-4 P.M., and 7-9 P.M. Monday-Sunday. Mrs. Burr McCarthy, R.N., Prop."

Jenny's stomach heaved. The sun shining on the metal sign was reflected into her eyes.

". . . father and I are going in here to talk to Mrs. McCarthy," Mrs. Pennoyer was saying. She touched her hair. "You girls can wait in the car for us. Or maybe you'd rather take Ethel out on the lawn."

Mr. Pennoyer pocketed the ignition key and pulled down the rearview mirror to check his appearance. He ran his hand over his hair. "We won't be long." He got out of the car.

Jenny tumbled out after them. "Wait, I'm coming with you—"

Her father stopped. "You don't want to come in here," he said.

Her mother looked up at the sky, then back at the car. "Gail," she called, "it's so nice. Take Ethel out, let her play on the lawn." Then to Jenny, "You help Gail watch Ethel."

"I'm coming with you. In there."

"Frank," Mrs. Pennoyer said. "Talk to your daughter."

Her father put his hand on his bald spot. "Jenny, there's nothing in there for you. Just a lot of old people. We're going to talk to Mrs. McCarthy, see what the place is like."

"It's for Grandpa," Jenny said. "You want to put him away in this place."

"Not put him away!" Mr. Pennoyer kicked at the

gravel. "We're thinking about this place for Grandpa to live. We heard good things about it. It's got an excellent reputation." He took a handkerchief out of his pocket and wiped his face. "I hear the food is first class."

"Oh, Dad—don't," Jenny said. "Please don't . . ."

Mr. Pennoyer folded his handkerchief, then stuffed it back into his pocket. "Now, listen, Jenny, it's my own father. I've got respect for him and I don't like this any better than you do, but it's got to be done. We can't consider just one man, we've got a whole family to think about. Now, why don't you go back to the car and wait for your mother and me?"

She followed them up the walk. Her father turned. "I'm telling you to quit this, Jenny. Stay out here. This has nothing to do with you."

"Grandpa has to do with me." She tried to speak softly. "I have to see this place. Don't you understand?" Despite herself, her voice rose, her cheeks swelled, and she was afraid she'd cry.

"Frank . . ." Her mother touched her father's arm. "Maybe it's a good idea for her to come in. Let her see. It's nice in there, she can see for herself we're only trying to do something good for Grandpa."

On the porch her father pressed the button on the side of the door. Jenny heard the chimes sound. Then a woman in a white uniform and white crepe-soled shoes opened the door. "Come in," she said, "it's visiting hours, you can walk right in. The door's always open."

"We want to speak to Mrs. McCarthy," Jenny's mother said. "We have an appointment." When she stood straight she was taller than Jenny's father. "It's about someone—a person—that is, my father-in-law, coming into the Home."

In the hall where they waited there were two high windows over the door, a staircase on one side, and on the other side a long row of metal hooks with coats and jackets hanging from them. Over each hook was a number. To the right there were double wooden doors, slightly ajar. Jenny looked into an enormously long room with tall windows, stuffed with couches, chairs, tables, and lamps. At the far end of the room several people clustered around a big color TV set showing a cowboy movie. In a gray upholstered chair, her head slumped down on her chest, a woman with sparse white hair was sleeping; near the door an old man wearing a plaid golfing cap and a bright red sweater was sitting with his hands folded. Seeing Jenny, he smiled.

"Hi," she said. There was a dim drowsy haze and hush in the room.

A woman in a white uniform walked up to Mr. Pennoyer and shook his hand. "How do you do? I am Mrs. Burr McCarthy." She had a scrubbed look and smelled of soap. "Won't you come into my office?" She held open a door that Jenny hadn't noticed before, and they filed in ahead of her.

Mrs. McCarthy sat down behind a desk littered with papers. "Sit down, please. Mrs. Pennoyer, take that chair. Make yourselves comfortable." Jenny stood beside the window that overlooked the porch.

"This is a lovely place," Mrs. Pennoyer said. "Even this room . . ."

Mrs. McCarthy sat ramrod straight behind her desk, her clean hands folded neatly on the desk. "We think we have an unusual Home. This house used to be part of the Westwood estate. It was built for the millionaire Cyrus Westwood—he made his money in toothpaste, you know. Very fine people. He had this house built to his exact specifications. I'm proud to say it's as sound as the day it was built. We have fifteen bedrooms in our Home, a large forty-foot living room, and a dining room that easily seats our entire Family. Now, I take it you're here to discuss a placement? A dear one you would like to bring into our Family?"

"My father," Mr. Pennoyer said, clearing his throat. "He's eighty-three, and he's getting on—"

"We've cared for him for thirteen years," Mrs. Pennoyer said. She wet her lips. "Lately, it's just getting to be too much."

"I understand," Mrs. McCarthy said. "Let me assure you that our people receive the best care here. I'm a registered nurse, I have two practical nurses on my staff, and we have the services of a physician. We meet all state standards of health care. Is your father senile?"

"No, he's not!" Jenny said.

"Jenny," her father said warningly.

"Well—he may be tending that way," Mrs. Pennoyer said.

"Of course. It's the age," Mrs. McCarthy said. "When we get that old, we all have to be looked after. Does he exhibit any strongly anti-social behavior such as temper tantrums, willfulness, or bedwetting?"

"He's not very strong," Mrs. Pennoyer said. "Has to be watched. It's a strain . . ." Her voice dropped off.

Mrs. McCarthy reached to one side of her desk and, opening a drawer, took out a long printed booklet. She handed it to Mr. Pennoyer. "In this booklet we explain our rules and standards of conduct for our Family. At the back you'll find a schedule of our rates."

Jenny's heart was beating frantically inside her chest. Until this moment she still hadn't quite believed it. Now it was real—as real as the printed booklet with the schedule of rates that her father was reading.

"Everyone in our Family has a complete health and personality file," Mrs. McCarthy said. She pointed to the large green file at her back. "We number code all our special diets. The chairs in the living room are numbered, so each resident has his own chair. It makes them feel more secure and cuts down on the bickering. I don't like bickering among my old people. I like them to be serene and happy in their twilight years. We like to think of this as a happy, happy place."

Mr. Pennoyer loosened his collar. "My father likes to take walks, read newspapers. He's actually very alert."

"Well, of course," Mrs. McCarthy said. "Everybody's

different. Some of our oldsters are happy playing cards, or watching TV, or knitting. We have writers here, too. Yes, we do! Mr. Munk writes letters to the papers every single day, and he's *so* expressive. And Mrs. Rothman is in the garden weeding and raking every chance she gets. We have some very active old people.

"Of course we have the others. You know, the ones who just sit. They're sweet, too. Some of them talk about things that happened so long ago as if those things are really happening right now. We don't object to that, if the resident is happy thinking that way, but sometimes we have to have reality therapy. For instance, one of our ladies, Mrs. Cloud, always likes to talk about her mother and the things her mother had given her. Well, that's harmless, you see, but when Mrs. Cloud began talking about her mother coming to visit, we decided she needed some reality therapy. Mrs. Cloud is ninety-two, so naturally her mother isn't visiting her. We told her firmly that her mother was dead, and we reminded her just when her mother died. I have all that information in my files."

Mrs. McCarthy cast a contented look at the metal cabinets. "If you decide to make your father one of our Family, then we'll ask you a lot of questions. His hobbies, interests, idiosyncrasies. All to help make his stay with us serene and happy." She stood up. "I hope I've answered most of your questions."

She led the way to the hall and they all followed her. "I think we'd like to see the facilities," Mrs. Pennoyer said. "Wouldn't we, Frank?"

From down the hall under the staircase there were kitchen sounds—pots clattering, water running—and in the air, the smell of creamed corn.

Mrs. McCarthy pushed the double wooden doors wide. "This is our living room, some of our modern folks call it the community room. Hello, everyone!" Her voice rose in pitch. "How are you, honey," she said to the white-haired woman that Jenny had noticed before. The woman blinked rapidly.

"Mrs. McCarthy, my son didn't come see me today. He promised he'd come."

Mrs. McCarthy patted her hand. "I'm sorry, honey. Did you enjoy the ice cream today? Did you ask for doubles, honey?" She moved on to an old man sitting in a chair with a wool plaid blanket across his legs. "How's my baby boy?" The old man had a big Adam's apple and thin knobby hands. Mrs. McCarthy took a tissue from her pocket and wiped his mouth. "Now you be a good boy," she said, "don't get the girls all fussed up the way you did yesterday."

She turned to Jenny's parents, smiling. "Yesterday, the bad old thing tried to kiss Mrs. Ellias. Can you imagine? They're like children. Naughty, naughty. We gave him a tranquilizer and calmed him right down." She gave her stiff white nurse's cap a pat and set it a bit straighter. "Notice we have a piano here, and we have games and books, and a tropical fish tank—that's the gift of one of the lovely families who have their mother here. We think this is one of the best-equipped community rooms in a rest home this size in the entire state. There's something here for everyone, and we're proud of that! Did you notice the large, clear picture on our color television? A lot of our residents have some eye trouble, fading eyesight, cataracts, and so forth and they couldn't see a small or dim picture."

"It's certainly a fine picture," Mr. Pennoyer said.

"I suppose you'd like to see the bedrooms," Mrs. McCarthy said. Mr. Pennoyer nodded. "Well, we are just as proud of them as we are of everything else in our home. They're on the second and third floors. We do have two bedrooms with several beds downstairs here for residents who can't make the climb, but generally we feel the climb is good for them. Keeps the circulation working and gives them exercise every day."

One of the women who'd been sitting on a couch quietly watching the TV suddenly bent over and began moaning. "Oh! Oh! Oh!"

Mrs. McCarthy went to her and patted her back.

"What is it, Bertha? Tell me what's bothering you."

The woman looked up at Mrs. McCarthy. She had high cheekbones and a prominent nose. "Get me out of here," she said. "Get me out of here!"

"Now, dear, you just calm down, you just be quiet and calm, honey. I'll send Miss Bird to give you something to help you relax."

"I don't want anything. Get me out of here. Get me out of here."

Mrs. McCarthy motioned the Pennoyers to leave and closed the double wooden doors.

"Bertha's been with us for, oh, ten years now," Mrs. McCarthy said. "She's a lovely lady. She was a schoolteacher, very refined, but she has her good days and her bad days like all of us. On her good days, I like to draw her out, get her to converse. Now let's go upstairs."

As Jenny started up after her parents and Mrs. McCarthy, Bertha began moaning once more. The sound came clearly through the wooden doors. The back of Jenny's neck went cold. She felt sick, sick. She hated this place and pitied every old person here. Her heart beat wildly and her leaden legs refused to carry her any farther up the stairs. She didn't want to see the bedrooms, to stare at any more inhabitants as if they were on display in a zoo, or hear Mrs. Burr McCarthy going on in her calm, sensible way about the "lovely" residents.

She turned and ran down the stairs, through the hall, past the numbered coat hooks and through the smell of creamed corn. Outside, Gail was playing with Ethel near the maple tree. She'd made a pile of leaves, and Ethel was sitting in the middle of it, crowing as Gail brushed leaves onto her. "Where's Mom and Dad," Gail called.

"Still inside."

"Is it nice there? It looks awfully nice."

There was a suffocating weight in Jenny's chest. After the days of gloom and rain, the sun seemed dazzlingly bright. Jenny threw herself down on the ground, pushing her face into the stiffness and crackle of grass and leaves. She had never felt so helpless in her life. She wanted to kick and scream as she had when she was a little girl, but she lay there, rigid and miserable, knowing the futility of it.

There was nothing she could do. Her parents would bring Grandpa here: they would say, *We're not forcing you, just see how you like it,* and then they would leave him. This was the way they had gotten him out of his apartment, and this was the way they would get him into the old people's home.

# *Chapter 15*

The old man walked slowly through the house, telling himself that he mustn't blame Jenny. Why expect her to be tied down, to stay home on a beautiful Sunday with him? He wasn't unreasonable. He understood. But all the same—the way she had rushed out without a word of goodbye, or "See you later, Grandpa."

He went into the kitchen, where Frankie was making himself a sandwich, spreading peanut butter on bread with his fingers. The old man thought about making himself a cup of tea. "What's the matter, Grandpa?" Frankie said. He sucked a gob of peanut butter off his finger. "You okay?" He came close to the old man, breathing peanut butter smells into his face. "What are you mumbling to yourself for? That's the way you do at night. You talk in your sleep all the time. Do you know that?"

Carl stiffened. Mumbling to himself! He pressed his lips firmly together, locking them against any more vagrant words, then walked out, trying to remember to stand straight, not to fumble at a chair for support through the dining room. Ever since the night of the grease fire, his faults and weaknesses had been exposed, probed, mercilessly discussed, and commented upon by everyone. It seemed that he had been living in a fool's paradise for years.

He had thought of himself as a strong, firm, intelligent, and clever man. He had imagined that his son felt reassured with him living in the house; his son could leave his family every morning knowing they were safe because Carl George Pennoyer was there. A strange gurgle escaped the old man, half-laugh, half-sob. He looked around quickly, afraid that Frankie might have heard him. Downstairs in his own home, he had been able to fumble, groan, talk out loud, make noises of all kinds, and there was no one around to hear or stare or laugh; no one to make it clear to him that he was an old, old nuisance of a man.

Nuisance. He said it aloud. "You're an old nuisance, Carl Pennoyer."

"You say something, Grandpa?" Frankie came to the door.

"Nothing." Nuisance. He said it again in his mind. The bitterness got no easier. He had sometimes in the past called himself an old fool, but he'd never really believed it. Now he was no longer sure of anything. Old fool, he accused himself. Old nuisance. Mumbler. Disturber of sleep. Clumsy old man. Useless creature!

His chest tightened, and he was shaken by a spasm of coughing that left him bent over, whistling for breath. His throat burned and he sat down in a chair, forgetting that he had planned to comb his hair and shine his shoes. He sat by the window, pretending to watch the TV show that Frankie had turned on. His thoughts drifted to the farm, where his grandfather had worked until the day he died. A curious feeling came over him, remembering that old man and then himself as a boy. He seemed to be at the narrow end of a very long tunnel, looking backward. There he was! Little Carl Pennoyer, big as life! And there was his grandfather, the old man, George Pennoyer, with his one good eye.

He felt curiously lightheaded and moved in the chair, only half aware that he was mumbling to himself again. He closed his eyes, snorting and sucking in his lips, a string of saliva dripping from the corner of his mouth. He was absorbed in remembering that golden, warm time of his childhood. Taking the trip upstate *. . . going to visit Grandpa, going to visit Grandpa . . .* It was a shrill childish cadence that brought a smile to his thin lips. He must have sung that himself, happy in the dusty train . . . *going to visit Grandpa* . . .

The old man, his grandfather, had had a dusty beard that smelled of hay, and a glass eye that had fascinated little Carl. Sitting in the wagon next to his grandfather, he had studied that glass eye . . . *Gee-up!* . . . A whip cracked, the big gray work horses, shoulder muscles bunched, moved forward, pulling little Carl and his grandfather, and in the wagon behind them, a load of coal for the winter months . . . the creaking wagon, the hot, good stink of fresh manure, the sun streaming down on them . . .

A car door slammed and voices rose. Carl's eyes opened. They were back. He groaned and groaned again. His neck ached. He must have fallen asleep. He pushed himself up from the chair.

In Frankie's room he lay down on the bed, his hands folded across his chest. He heard the family come in. Let Jenny look for him. Let her see that he was lying there on the bed peacefully, indifferent and uncaring that she had left him all afternoon to go on a drive with her mother and father.

"Grandpa?" Jenny came to the door. "Grandpa, are you sleeping?"

He didn't answer. Have some pride, he told himself, and he lay there, mouth sucked in, saying nothing, having his pride. Jenny left, and he fumbled a blanket from the foot of the bed over his shoulders.

An hour later Jenny was at the door again. "Grandpa, I'm eating supper with you tonight."

The old man opened his eyes. "That so?" (Every night now he fixed his own supper, put it on a tray, brought it into Frankie's room—he'd never call it his room, never—and sat in the Boston rocker, eating alone.) He wondered at Jenny's being given permission to eat with him. Frank was a fanatic about his family being present at the table with him.

"Sit up, Grandpa," Jenny said, putting a tray down on the bureau. "I fixed everything myself." Her voice was muffled, and the old man thought she was suffering pangs of conscience for having left him that afternoon. Graciously, he decided to forgive her. They shared toast, tea, buttered noodles, pears, and slices of American cheese. With Jenny to keep him company, the food tasted sweet. His sweet Jenny. He frowned. He'd forgiven her for deserting him that afternoon, but maybe he should have said something. Maybe she didn't realize. She was eating almost as little as he, poking at her food. And her eyes—red, swollen, blinking continually, as if irritated by sand.

"Jenny." He reached to touch her hand, but didn't. He wasn't a touching person. "Jenny, child, tell Grandpa," he said, echoing all the times when she'd been four or five or six and had come crying to him. "Tell Grandpa." Grandpa would fix. Grandpa would make better.

She looked up, gulped for air, pushed away the tray. Her eyes filled with tears and she rushed out of the room. He sat still, defeated again, sour, puzzled, and helpless. Grandpa couldn't fix anything. He sat there for a long time, unmoving, And then she was back. She came in, closed the door, and knelt in front of him, her head on his knees.

"Grandpa. I must tell you. They're going to send you to a Home. That's where they went today. They said they'll talk to you about it, and take you to visit. But I know they'll leave you there. They'll say, 'Just see how you like it, Grandpa,' and they'll leave you there." It all came out in a choking rush, half-whispered, fearful, pleading.

The old man felt his strength draining as she spoke, felt himself going weak with fear. "Go away," he said. He pushed her aside and stumbled to the bed.

He lay there a long time—all that night, the next day, and the next night, and he thought of nothing else but what Jenny had told him. The family came to the door—his son, his daughter-in-law, the children. *Grandpa*, they said, *what's the matter? Are you sick again? Grandpa, don't you want to get up?*

He didn't answer. He thought he would die. They were sending him to a Home . . . one of those places . . . putting him away . . . into the garbage heap . . . useless old fool . . . old horses go for glue . . old men aren't even good for that . . .

He thought of the day when he was told not to cross streets alone. That day, he ought to have gone out and, like Moses parting the Red Sea, walked into the middle of the worst traffic on Pittmann Street. (Once he'd seen a man, an accident victim, lying at the edge of the road, covered with a sheet, bare feet sticking out. Down the road a bit were his shoes, neatly side by side, as if waiting for the owner to step into them.)

Why had he listened to them? Why had he let them lead him upstairs? Why had he taken those first steps? Slept on the couch. Agreed to move into his grandson's bedroom while they painted and cleaned. Didn't he know, even then, that they'd never let him move back down? *Ah, Grandpa,* they'd said, *it's better this way, up here we can help you, be with you . . .*

And that was when the real weakness began, the awful weakness, the feeling of bones turned to liquid, legs barely able to support his large, useless body. Overnight he had become sick and old. Had made their prophecies come true. And now this.

His mind reeled away from the thought of a home for old people. He had wanted to die like his grandfather! On his feet and busy to the last day.

He got up to go to the bathroom, clinging to the walls as he made his way through the house. His ears rang and in the bathroom he wanted to weep as he made his water. Even his water was feeble. Oh, he was old, so old and helpless, and no one cared.

That night, worn out by fears and thoughts and self-pity, he slept very deeply. When he woke Wednesday morning with the sun shining in through the window, his mind felt calm as a pool of water. He sat up, thinking, *I will go away.* The idea came to him complete—where he would go, what he would do, how he would do it. The farm, of course. He tested the thought, turning it around and around in his mind, then tested himself, swinging his legs over the side of the bed, groaning automatically, but feeling the blood moving through his body, feeling himself coming alive. I will go away! He closed the window with a vigorous bang.

"Grandpa!" Frankie yelped from the top bunk and buried his head under the pillow.

He went to the bathroom and washed briskly in cold water, snuffling and snorting with enjoyment. In his excitement he thought at first that he would go that very day, put on his old black coat and walk away. But, as he'd always been sensible, he told himself that Saturday would be time enough. He would spend a few days preparing.

# Chapter 16

Jenny woke to hear Ethel rattling the bars of her crib. "Ja!" she cried. "Ja! Up!" There was the sound of water running, a toilet flushing, and then her father yelling that he couldn't find his blue shirt.

Jenny dressed slowly, her fingers clumsy on the buttons. Ever since she had told Grandpa about the Home, she had felt this way, frightened and despairing, heavy with clumsiness and fear. Had she thought he would rise up and find a way to defy them? She had been wrong, terribly totally wrong.

In the bathroom she splashed water on her face, combed her hair, scratched a scab off her knee, putting off the moment when she had to join the family for breakfast. None of them knew how she felt—alone, separate, apart from them. The day before she had tried to talk to her parents. *You can't do this to Grandpa. What do you mean, can't* her father had said. His neck reddened. *Dad, please, a Home—it's, it's monstrous. Monstrous,* he said. *Jenny, what a fine way you have of talking. A fine way to call your parents monsters. No, we're not monsters,* he said, *but there are some things in life that have to be faced. You'll know when you get older. You wait and see, it's going to be a good thing for him. No,* she'd said, *no, no.* And her mother had put her hand out toward Jenny, saying, *You'll be able to visit him weekends, every weekend, spend time with him, it'll be better all around . . .*

Jenny slowly hung the towel over the rod. Gail was

banging on the door. "What are you DOING in there?" she cried. "Jenny, answer me! Will you get out, please?"

Jenny opened the door, and Gail pushed past her. "You'll make me late for school!"

Jenny went back to their room and took Ethel out of her crib. The child's damp, warm weight was comforting. She pushed her nose into the milky smelling hair and jiggled her as she carried her into the kitchen. Her mother was at the stove, wearing house slippers and a blue apron over her nightgown. And Grandpa, shaved and fully dressed, was standing by the sink drinking a cup of steaming tea.

"Grandpa!" Jenny said in pure astonished joy to find him looking just as he'd looked so many mornings of her life. As if he'd never been sick, never lain in the bunk bed, shrunken and yellow, looking as frail as if a gust of wind would blow his bones to the corners of the earth.

"Morning, Jenny," he said.

Her father entered, unwrapping the newspaper and folding it first to the full-page ad for the Big K Supermarket. On his heels came Frankie, sleepy-eyed, then Gail, with Coke cans in her hair. With all of them there, Jenny couldn't ask Grandpa what had happened, how the miracle had occurred: he was himself again!

That afternoon when she got home from school, anxious to see Grandpa, he wasn't sitting in the chair by the window or lying on the bottom bunk, or even shuffling up and down in front of the house. "He's been gone all afternoon," her mother said. "Said he was going out for a little walk, and it's three hours! I've been worrying all that time. The man has no thought for anyone! I went around the block with Ethel, looking for him, and he's nowhere in sight. No doubt he's got himself lost or worse. He's been so confused lately. If your father comes home and has to go out in the car and look for Grandpa, he's not going to like that one bit at the end of a hard day."

"I'll look for him," Jenny said. Her mother had her worried. She stepped out on the front porch. Cars were massed in both directions, horns blasting, exhausts panting. Had Grandpa really looked like himself this morning? She could easily have been mistaken and seen what she wanted to see. As she walked toward the Rimbauds she couldn't help looking at the spot on the street where Nicky had been killed. Was that oily smear of blood still there? A shudder passed through her. *Confused,* her mother said. *Lost.* What if he'd done the thing her mother had worried about—stepped out into traffic?

She looked down Catherine Street. He wasn't there. He could be anywhere in the city. He'd been gone three hours. Right now he might be lying on the side of a road. She hurried toward Fifth, shaded her eyes, and saw him. He was walking toward her, hands in the pockets of his limp-hemmed black coat. "Grandpa!" she called, waving her hands. She ran toward him. He stopped and waited for her. "Where were you? Where've you been?" she said. There were two high spots of color on his bony cheeks.

"Walking," he said.

"Walking? Where? Mom says you've been gone three hours. She was worried. You told her you were only going out for a little walk, hours ago."

Breathing hard, he looked at her over his steel spectacles. "I'll apologize to your mother," he said. His manner was entirely gracious. His hooded eyes were clear.

Jenny walked alongside him. "You feel good, don't you?" she said happily. "Did you go any place special? Were you down by the canal?"

"No," he said, "just walking. Getting out the kinks."

Jenny noticed the edge of a road map sticking out of his pocket. It was the kind given free at service stations. "What's that for? What's it a map of?" she asked, reaching for it.

He fended off her hand. "Me to know and you to wonder."

He went up the steps to their house, moving quite briskly. Jenny followed, happy and dazed. He was her own Grandpa again, brisk, curt, commanding. Would they dare send him to the Home when he was so splendid?

"So there you are," her mother said.

"Just lost track of time," he said. "Sorry, Amelia—"

Mrs. Pennoyer cut him off. "You had me worried half to death! I was thinking of calling the police to look for you."

"No need to worry about me," he said.

"*Isn't* there? Jenny, set the table now."

Jenny, automatically counting silver, answered her own question. Yes, they would dare send him to the Home. There would be a lot of talk about "senior citizens" and people who were "failing" in their later years. No matter if he entered on his own two feet or on a stretcher, one way or the other Grandpa was going to the Home.

# Chapter 17

Going into Frankie's room, the old man lay down on his bunk bed, overheated and sweating. His mouth was dry. He needed a drink of water, but he had to rest first. He had barely gotten to the room without showing Amelia the weakness and trembling in his legs. He rubbed his kneecaps. His legs felt like stretched-out rubber bands.

*You fool, old man,* he said in his mind, *you do nothing for weeks, then walk five miles in one afternoon.* But he felt pleased, triumphant. He had tested himself, walked fifty city blocks. He had counted them, letting the numbers ring in his head as they added up. Ten! E-leven! . . . Twenty-one! . . . Thirty-four! . . . And pushed himself to forty-six, forty-seven, forty-eight, forty-nine, fifty! Fifty city blocks. Five miles. Not bad for an old, sick man. Not bad at all. Sick? Ha! Tomorrow he would walk again, walk out the aches in his muscles and in his back. Walk with his chin set into the wind, hands behind his back, aware of everything in the world.

Fifty blocks. Five miles. True, he'd had to stop, rest, catch his breath, but he'd done it. He rubbed his knees. Aching. He didn't care. He could do it. Could walk away from all the hypocrisy and disrespect. Didn't have to bend his neck to any man. He thought of the farm and it was like thinking of God. Blue light before dawn . . . cows complaining deeply . . . wet grass covering bare feet . . .

He'd been young there once—young, strong, happy.

He'd never be that young again, but he wasn't as old and weak and sick as they'd been telling him. The weakness that had made his legs tremble and his voice quiver had come from defeat and fear, from believing that he was as helpless and cracked as they said. A man didn't have to be that old.

# Chapter 18

Jenny offered Ethel a spoonful of strained applesauce. "Delicious, honey," she coaxed and stuffed the spoon in Ethel's mouth. Ethel opened her mouth and let the applesauce trickle down her chin onto the highchair tray. "Ethel, you ought to be feeding yourself," Jenny said. Ethel grinned, put her hands into the spit-out applesauce, then brought all ten gloppy fingers into her mouth. "Very pretty," Jenny said. "You want to eat that way? Be my guest." She dumped the rest of the applesauce on Ethel's tray and went back to her bedroom to find sneakers and socks.

Dressed, her Saturday housework done, Jenny knocked on Frankie's closed door. "Grandpa?" she called. But only her mother was in the room, washing the woodwork. "Where's Grandpa?"

Her mother wrung out her soapy rag over the yellow plastic bucket. "He went out a few minutes ago. Said he was going to take a walk again. That man! We're going to find him sick on the streets one of these days. What if he falls down? What is all this walking? What is the purpose of it? Every time he goes out I worry that he'll get sick, or lose his way, or be hit by a car."

Jenny had heard all that before. She wasn't worried about any of it, but a twinge of fear touched her. Why had Grandpa gone out without her? They had always walked together on Saturdays, and now that he was well again . . . Didn't he remember that today was Saturday? "Can I go now?" she said, tapping her foot impatiently. "I'm done with my work. I did everything you said."

"Not so fast, young lady. Bring me four sheets and two pillow cases from the linen closet. Not the new flowered ones, the blue muslin ones on the third shelf. Did you hear me, Jenny?"

"Yes, yes, I heard," Jenny said over her shoulder. A feverish feeling was building inside her, a thought that she was groping for, an idea eluding her. There was something about Grandpa and all of this walking, this sudden energy after his sickness, and the secretive, pleased smile that had flitted over his face several times in the past days. And then that road map she'd seen him studying . . .

She brought her mother the linen and laid it on the bureau. "Can I go now?" She shifted from foot to foot until her mother nodded.

In her bedroom she tied on a scarf and tore her jacket from the closet, sending a hanger clattering to the floor. For three days now, Grandpa had gone walking for hours and would say nothing about it, not even to her. *Where'd you go, Grandpa? Oh, just walking. Walking? See anything? Nothing much, nothing much.* And then that odd little smile that made Jenny want to smile too, but at the same time puzzled and teased her. Where is he going? What's he doing? Where is he now? Where? That smile . . . as if he were going to do something special. . . . She stood stock still in the middle of the room, nearly quivering. He was going away! Going away and not coming back, not going to the Home. That was it. That was the meaning of that sly cat smile. He wasn't going to be led to any Home!

She laughed, wanted to spin around and scream with joy. Grandpa! Grandpa! Good for you! Oh, wonderful!

Then it struck her—he was going away without her. Without having said goodbye, leaving her behind. Oh, no, he couldn't be allowed to do that. She wouldn't let him. She would find him, go with him. Wherever it was that he was going, she would go, too.

"Jenny, did you go out yet?" her mother called from Frankie's room.

She dug in her drawer, tossing aside underwear and socks, gathering up the bills and coins she threw in there whenever she babysat or had money left from her allowance.

"Jenny, come here, please, I have something else I want you to do."

She didn't answer, shoved the money in her pockets and moved quickly through the house. "Jenny, didn't you hear me?" her mother called.

For a moment she was drawn by the command in her mother's voice, then she opened the front door and went quickly down the porch steps. On the sidewalk, she wondered which way to go. Then she remembered the direction he'd come from on Tuesday—Fifth Street. Try that. At the corner of Fifth and Grove Avenue, the bus for downtown stopped.

She walked rapidly, dodging around the clumps of kids playing hopscotch and jump rope, whizzing up and down on their bikes. "Hey, Pennoyer," a boy called. A truck rumbled past, dripping oil. She felt impatient and scared. What if she didn't catch him? What if he hadn't gone this way at all? She began to run. Frankie had told her that jogging was better than running at top speed; if you were in shape and hit the right pace you could jog indefinitely. At the corner of Fifth she turned, and it occurred to her that this was the route Grandpa used to take to the tobacco store on Lyons Avenue.

Could buying tobacco be the big secret? That cat smile passed through her mind. No, it was more important than tobacco. Her feet slapped the sidewalk—heels first, Frankie had said, heels first, don't run on your toes. Her hair flew out behind her, she was hot, and wanted to throw off her jacket. "Oh, look at her run," someone said. There was a pebble in one of her sneakers, and the wind, shifting, blew grit into her mouth. Then, as she passed South Street, she saw Grandpa ahead of her, moving slowly in his long black coat. She came up behind him and like a child clutched him around the waist.

"Grandpa! Where are you going? Wait for me. I'm coming with you."

He disengaged her hands. He didn't look pleased. "Go home, Jenny."

She shook her head. "You're going someplace, aren't you? Someplace away, you're going away."

"What?" he said. "What?"

"You heard me, Grandpa! Don't be like that," she pleaded. "Tell me where you're going. I want to come with you. Wherever it is, we'll go together."

"Don't be foolish, child." A city bus was approaching and he stepped out on the curb and waved his hand to stop it. The doors swung open and he climbed stiffly up the steps. Jenny followed, dropped her coins into the box, and found a seat directly behind him.

"Go home," he said, without looking at her. "Next stop you get off."

"No," she said. She could be as stubborn as he was. She sat back, arms folded, her mouth set tightly.

He didn't say anything again until the bus jerked to a halt to pick up more passengers. "Now," he said without looking at her. "Off. You can get a bus home across the street. Shoo! Scat! Scram!"

"Stop yelling at me," she said into his ear. "People are looking. And save your breath, Grandpa, you can't get rid of me. That's that." A woman in a green and blue plaid coat sat down next to Jenny, and Jenny leaned back in the seat. Gears ground, the bus lumbered away from the curb, and the sickening smell of exhaust fumes drifted through the interior.

"They won't let you," Grandpa said, three streets

later, throwing the words over his shoulder. It was his first admission that she was right, that he was going away.

Jenny leaned forward. "I'm not asking their permission," she said fiercely. The woman in the plaid coat was looking at her curiously. Jenny glanced out the smudged window, only half seeing the city moving by. Where was Grandpa going? She imagined the two of them living in another city, a room together, taking care of each other. Could they do it? Grandpa didn't have much money, she had to go to school . . .

"Alliance, Common Center," the bus driver yelled, jerking the bus to a halt. "End of line. All out." Jenny moved forward behind Grandpa, down the metal steps, out onto the street. Downtown was packed sidewalks, the smell of caramel corn and bus exhaust, a policeman's whistle cutting sharply through the moist air.

"Across the street, Pittmann Street bus," Grandpa said, pointing with his chin.

"All right, suppose I go home. Then where are you going?"

"Now, Jenny, I'm not going to say. I don't want them coming after me."

"Grandpa." She was deeply hurt. "I would never tell. Never."

He looked at her, faded eyes considering her, then nodded. "The farm," he said.

"Oh!" Of course! The farm. She had heard about it so often, imagined it so vividly—the turkeys, the cows, Grandpa's grandfather with his funny glass eye. But of course all that was gone now. Still—"Grandpa, that's a wonderful idea." She hugged his arm as they walked. "I can go there with you. We'll both go."

"No," he said roughly.

"What are you going to do there?"

"Live," he said simply.

"Alone?"

"Alone."

"No, you're not. I'll live with you."

"Ha! What will you do there? A child."

"Stop that, Grandpa. I'm not a baby. I'll live with you, go to school, help you—we'll be together."

He crossed Adams Street, into the sun. A car coming too fast around the corner headed straight for him. There was a furious horn blast. Jenny grabbed her grandfather's arm and pulled him back. As the driver sped past, he showed an upraised fist and yelled "Stupid old man!"

They threaded through the cars and walked on the sidewalk again. Then into the bus depot, a dirty brick building smelling of dried fish and bathroom cleanser.

"This is as far as you go," Grandpa said. He went to the ticket counter. "One way to New Sayre." He pulled bills out of his pocket, wet his fingers, and counted them slowly.

The ticket agent counted the money again. "Nineteen fifty-eight, just right, old man," he said. "Bus leaves in half an hour."

Jenny moved up. "One way to New Sayre." She glanced at Grandpa. "I've got money," she said. She had twenty-one dollars. She spilled coins and bills on the counter. Grandpa watched her from the side, his mouth working silently. She took her ticket, put it in her jacket pocket and followed him to a bench.

"They'll worry about you," he said.

"You, too."

He snorted. "Don't be foolish. They'll be glad to be rid of me." He fingered his ticket. "Bring your ticket back; tell the man you made a mistake."

She set her mouth stubbornly, sat more firmly on the bench. She wouldn't let any questions, ifs, ands, or buts, intrude into her mind. If he was going, she was going. Without him at home, she didn't want to be home. It was that simple.

"Bus for Hamilton, Freeland, Cambridge, Bundysburg, New Lyme, and New Sayre now loading at the West Gate." The metallic voice echoed through the room. "Bus for Hamilton, Freeland, Cambridge . . ."

Grandpa stood up, mouth working. "West Gate . . ."

Jenny pointed to the West Gate exit. "Over there, Grandpa." A crowd had collected. The bus, panting like a huge beast, slowly swallowed the people. "Get your money back," Grandpa said, shuffling forward with the crowd. "Still time."

Jenny pressed closer to him. "Now stop picking your nose," a woman exclaimed, slapping her little boy's hand. A girl with a knapsack on her back smiled. A young couple leaned on each other, kissing intently. The bus gulped, swallowed, the crowd shrank.

"Far enough. Let's stop this. You leave now," Grandpa said.

"I'm not leaving, Grandpa." She took her ticket from her pocket.

He turned, old man's mouth thin, sour. "I have no authority with anyone. Not even you!" His mouth worked over the words.

Jenny fell back. "Do you really want me to go?" Her throat ached. "Grandpa—" She grabbed the roughness of his coat. "Don't you understand?" A smell of mothballs and stale tobacco rose from the coat. "Grandpa, I can't leave you. I love you."

Someone behind pushed her in the small of her back. "Move. You're holding up the line." She shuffled forward, still clutching Grandpa's coat, then released him to go up the metal steps of the bus.

# *Chapter 19*

The old man leaned back in his seat, eyes closed, giving himself to the throbbing motion of the moving bus. It was good to be sitting down again. The strain and excitement of the morning, of actually leaving, of arguing with Jenny, had tired him. But now he was on his way to the farm. Behind his eyelids, golden lights danced. He saw vast fields of green and yellow, a white house with black shutters, a red barn, a cow standing by a barbed wire fence, tall maples shedding a soft green shade over a comfortable front porch with an oak-slatted swing moving in the breeze. That was the way the farm had looked years ago when he was a child. Seventy-five years ago.

Tenanted, and then empty since that time, the place would have run down, would need repairs. But it was a house, a real home, a place where he could be independent, care for himself. Depend on no one else. He had his social security check every month. He'd grow his own food (squash, potatoes, carrots, cabbage —all things he could store in bushel baskets through the winter in the cold cellar). He'd heat with wood and coal; buy a cow, milk her twice a day; add a few chickens for eggs.

He shook his head in wonderment. Why had he waited so many years? Oh, yes, he remembered—Frances had hated the country, the silence, the smell of manure, the dusty roads. When Frances died, he might have gone to the farm, but there had been tenants on the place. Then, when they left, three years later,

Jenny was firmly in his life. He could no more have left her than cut off his right arm. But now he had to go.

He stirred, feeling the scratchy fabric of the seat at his neck. He opened his eyes enough to see her sitting next to him, looking out the window. He'd meant it when he tried to send her back. It wasn't his idea to take her away from her family. But what could he do? She'd followed him, stubbornly insisted she was going with him. Where had she got that stubborn quality? From him, likely. The way he felt, he'd had as much to do with her upbringing, her character, as anyone. And he was proud of her. Not that he'd ever tell her —what for? So she could get a swelled head?

He decided he'd let her come along for a few days, then send her back. Or maybe—might Frank allow her to live with him? He toyed with the idea, thinking of his son, feeling a knot in his chest at the memory of his son's betrayal. He got out his pipe, clamped it in his mouth, chewed on the stem. No need getting upset over his son anymore. There wasn't going to be any Home for him. No home but his own home.

## Chapter 20

*What the hell were you thinking of?* Jenny could hear her father's voice in her ear. *Running off with Pop. Are you as crazy as he is?*

She pressed her face against the window. They had left Alliance behind them, were passing through Grigg's Corners. Wire link fences separated the slashing throughway from the geometric rows of neat houses and trim yards. A little boy teetering on a bike waved at the bus which thundered along the highway, dwarfing the cars. Mile markers flashed by. Jenny caught glimpses of other lives, other places: a woman on her stoop shaking out a dust mop . . . a long, dirty brick factory pouring columns of white and black smoke into the air . . . a dead dog, bloody and stiffened by the side of the highway . . . a billboard picture of a girl with a dazzling smile holding up a bottle of liquor . . .

The bus hummed with the solid smacking hum of tires on pavement, with the softer buzzing of people talking. In the seat ahead, a child dozed on her mother's lap. Had she ever leaned that way against her mother, so safe and comfortable? She thought she must have, but couldn't remember. Her mother would be furious, too. *Jenny, Jenny, must you always do things your own way!* She moved closer to Grandpa, felt his bony leg next to hers.

Cars raced the highway in packs. She saw license plates from half a dozen states. "Look, there's one from Arizona," she said. She and Gail used to make lists of out-of-state license plates.

"I can remember when roads were empty," Grandpa said. "Stretched for miles, grand and empty. Nearly seventy years ago. Made my way on foot and by thumb through twenty states. I could walk in the middle of the road without fear, not any superhighways then. If a farmer came along, he'd give me a ride in his wagon."

In Jenny's mind that trip of Grandpa's, when he'd been not much older than she, had always had the sound of birds flying. So free and beautiful. Moving down one road, and up another, lifting his face to the rain or the sun, working when he was hungry, sleeping where he could, in fields or barns.

Under the wheels of the bus, the road flew by, a mile quicker than a minute. A day's walk of seventy years ago passed now in less than half an hour. Outside the bus windows the world raced by. Frozen pictures. A school, white shades half drawn . . . three squat yellow buses lettered in black, "Rexboro Central Sc" . . . a cluster of lollipop houses, green, pink, blue . . . a factory looking like a long stone coffin, dead face turned to the highway . . . a grocery store, metal sign swinging . . .

What would her parents do when she didn't show up for supper? Call Rhoda first. Then other friends. Then the police? She didn't want them to worry. She'd let them know she was all right, but not yet. Not until Grandpa was safe at the farm. Not until she was sure they couldn't come and get him, take him to the Home. Her arms got goosepimply. The Home. She didn't want to think about it. Grandpa wasn't going there.

A State Police car moved smoothly past the bus. Jenny looked down at it, felt a lump of fear in her stomach. Looking for them? For her and Grandpa? She half exepected the siren to wind up, the bus to pull over to the shoulder, the state trooper to board.

*I'm looking for an old man and a runaway girl . . .*

She forced herself to watch the scenery flashing past. Roads slashing through the countryside . . . cemetery of white mobile homes . . . Hughes Mills, a cluster of a dozen houses . . . gas stations with flags . . . parking lot crammed with row upon row of glittering cars . . . towns and villages . . . Carpenters Falls . . . Whitesboro . . . Rochester . . . Falksburg . . . Big Rock . . . houses . . . stores . . . factories . . . Her mind blurred. She leaned back, slept.

# *Chapter 21*

At Hamilton they got out, stretched, looked around. It might have been Alliance. Cars packed tight, dirty streets, boys in jeans and long hair in front of the bus station. Inside the terminal Grandpa had a drink of water, and Jenny bought a bag of hard candies. They used the bathrooms, stretched, got back on the bus.

They settled into their seats, already made homelike with their coats, a newspaper Grandpa had bought, candy wrappers, a crumpled plastic cup. Jenny combed her hair. The driver walked up the aisle, checking tickets. There were little settling sounds all around. The bus humped forward. They passed through tiny villages, sprawling suburbs, cities choked with smoke and soot. The trip took on a dulling sameness, punctuated only by occasional stops for the bathroom and snacks.

As they passed through town after town they dozed in their seats. Between naps Grandpa told Jenny of the fifteen-year-old Carl Pennoyer and the things he'd seen and done on his great trip. "Slept under a schoolhouse," he said, "with the smell of cats in my nose . . . saw blacks living in teepees like Indians . . . worked on a farm picking beans, another farm picking strawberries . . . I was even bit once by a black widow spider and lived to tell the story." The world outside was a blur of darkness broken by headlights flashing past on the highway. The night bus was only half full, the lights were dimmed, and all around them people slept. Jenny's eyes felt heavy as sand; she hoped the bus driv-

er didn't feel as hypnotized as she by the sighing of
the tires, the dimness of the interior, and the soft
*whoosh! whoosh! whoosh!* of cars passing.

When she woke her mouth was gritty and her eyes
itched as if someone had thrown dirt into them. She
sat up, sighing and blinking. It was nearly dawn. The
bus entered a small town, slowed down, and came to
a groaning stop in front of a tightly closed store.
"New Sayre," the driver said. His face looked waxy.
"New Sayre," he said again.

"Grandpa." Jenny shook him. "We're here. In New
Sayre, I mean."

# Chapter 22

The town smelled of manure. It was five o'clock in the morning. After the continual throbbing of the bus, the quietness of New Sayre was almost jarring to their senses.

"Now we walk," Grandpa said. He flexed his fingers and moved slowly up and down the empty sidewalk, kneading his arms and shoulders, groaning under his breath.

"How far is the farm?" Jenny asked.

"Eight miles. Too early to find anyone to give us a ride."

Jenny looked around New Sayre curiously. A water pump was set on a concrete base in the middle of four intersecting streets. There were neat clapboard houses . . . a limestone church . . . a grocery store advertising local cheese . . . and a hardware store with bikes, snowmobiles, gas lanterns, and a set of plastic dishes in the window.

They began walking. In moments, they had left the sidewalks behind and were into farm country. They'd walk, Grandpa said, till they came to another church, then a turn-off onto Honeywell Road, past a cemetery, and keep going till they came to Turkey Hill Road.

The sky brightened slowly and a milky blue light spread upward from the horizon. Pockets of fog lay in the low places. Somewhere cows moaned mournfully, and a herdsman called. Otherwise, silence. Everywhere, silence. It was like being in church, Jenny thought, when being in church was just right, perfect.

They passed still houses with the shades drawn, cars parked watchfully near, their windows silvered with moisture. Only the faint sound of their shoes crunching on the road marred the perfect silence. Jenny didn't even want to talk. She moved easily at Grandpa's pace, puffing out her breath, looking everywhere, aware of a rising sense of excitement and freshness. The moment when she had thrown herself down on the lawn of the old people's home in utter, blank despair seemed very far away. Her parents, Pittmann Street, and Valerie and Vince she thought of with a kind of distant generosity. Let them have their apartment and their selfish disregard for Grandpa. What did she care now? She and Grandpa were here, on the way to the farm. They might as well have been in another world, on another planet—she felt that safe, that contented.

In a long green barn, lights showed in every window. "Farmer's up, milking," Grandpa said. The silence was punctuated now by the call of a bird, a long clean trill on two notes. Another bird answered. "What bird is that, I wonder?" Jenny said.

"Whitethroat," Grandpa said.

They passed another house. Lights shone through white curtains. A window was filled with plants. "Folks getting up, the day's starting," Grandpa said. A black dog came tearing out from behind the house, barking as if she had a mind to chew them both into little pieces. She followed them down the road. Jenny hopskipped a bit nervously. "Just letting us know who's boss," Grandpa said.

At a produce stand a woman in orange pajamas yawned behind the open-air counter. Jenny's stomach rumbled as they bought bananas, beans, tomatoes, and corn. Jenny tied food into her scarf and stuffed her jacket pockets. Bananas stuck out of Grandpa's coat pockets. She stripped an ear of corn, threw away the green and the silk, and chewed on it. Grandpa sucked a tomato.

They had walked for nearly an hour when a pickup truck stopped and a man put his head out the window. "You folks want a ride? Just going a few miles down the road, but be glad to give you a lift."

Grandpa got in front, while Jenny climbed into the open back, where a boy with slicked-down black hair was sitting on the floor. She sat down across from him. "Hi," she said. The boy nodded.

The truck jolted forward. "How old are you?" he asked. "I'm twelve," he went on without waiting for an answer. "Bet you thought I was older. Everyone thinks I'm older." He raised his voice to be heard over the sound of the motor. "I do whatever I want, drive my father's tractor, smoke, drink beer." He took a cigarette from the pocket of his plaid shirt and stuck it in the corner of his mouth. "You want one?" he asked Jenny.

She shook her head.

"You don't smoke?"

"No."

"Do you drink beer?"

"No."

The boy laughed. "Bet you don't do anything."

The truck turned in at a farm. A tractor stood in the rutted driveway. A half-filled wire corn crib leaned next to the barn. Jenny and the boy hopped off the back of the truck. "Very much obliged," Grandpa said, getting out.

"You say you folks are going to Turkey Hill Road?" the farmer asked. He rested his arms on the window of the truck.

Grandpa nodded. "The old Pennoyer place."

The man screwed his eyes up against the light, thinking.

"Pennoyer place," he said. "That would be that farm hasn't been lived on for quite a while."

"My place," Grandpa said. "Haven't been there for years. Plan to take up residence there now."

"You and the girl?" the farmer said. He looked at

his son. "Just you two?" He scratched his cheek as if trying not to laugh. "Going to live there, huh?" And again he scratched his cheek, his face twitching with laughter. "Well," he said to his son, "you hear something strange and wonderful every day, don't you?"

## Chapter 23

Jenny had expected a sign to announce Turkey Hill
Road, but there was only a rutted dirt road nearly
hidden by trees.

"Turn here," Grandpa said.

"This is it?" she said.

Grandpa nodded. "Two more miles."

The road was uphill. They climbed slowly and
steadily; fields opened on both sides, and above them
was a great wide sky. Jenny had never seen a sky that
looked so pure and blue, so freshly washed. In the
hard rocky shoulder of the road, growing things, green
things, had pushed through the unpromising earth.
"Every living thing wants its bit of space," Grandpa
said. As they moved along, the road became less of a
road and more of a path, rutted, rocky, and not easy
to walk on.

At the crest, there was another hill to climb. Grandpa was breathing hard and sat down by the side of the
road to rest. His hand trembling slightly, he unbut-
toned his coat. His face was coated with a faint sheen
of perspiration and he coughed several times. Taking
his aspirin bottle from his coat pocket, he shook three
tablets into his palm and chewed them.

They rested a few minutes and then started up the
second hill. Cows jostled around a wagon loaded with
green hay. A wave of blackbirds swooped down on
a field of corn stubble. "Almost there," Grandpa said,
breathing hard again. A blue jay complained in a
voice like rusty metal. "Skereeen! Skreen! Skreen!"

Grandpa pointed to a crabapple tree at the side of the road, its limbs bent over with clusters of small red fruit, and then to a row of tumbled fence posts. "Here's where my property starts, Jenny. See that field over there, and that hill, and the field beyond that? That's all Pennoyer land."

"All of that?" She had seen farms as the family sped past in the car, but she'd had no sense of size. The land Grandpa pointed to was bigger than Jericho Hill Park, where there were always dozens and dozens of people. Here there were only Grandpa and her, the hills, the clean blue sky, and the incredible stillness.

The road leveled, and Jenny wanted to run, but held back for Grandpa. His breathing was hard. They rounded a bend in the road and there, facing them, was a weathered ruin of a barn, silver-sided and sagging into the ground. "That's my barn," Grandpa said. "We're here." He stopped, his hand to his chest. "We're here," he said again.

There was a gaping opening where wooden doors had once slid along metal tracks. Jenny stepped in, sniffing a musty, stale odor. She had an impression of dimness, straw underfoot, patches of sky caught in a crisscross of broken, roofless beams. A thick rope dangled from a beam, coils of rusty barbed wire were everywhere, and so was the pungent sour smell of animals. A narrow wooden ladder leaned against a loft filled with tumbled dirty hay. "We're here!" Jenny cried. Her voice echoed back to her. She ran to the ladder, grasped a rung, and began climbing.

"Jenny!" Grandpa was in the doorway, outlined against the brightness. "Come down from there. Those rungs may be rotten."

"All right," she said, but for a long moment she held on with one hand, leaning out into the space over the barn floor, happy and strong. They were here. They had made it, the two of them together. Grandpa was safe.

Coming out of the barn, they crossed the road to

the house. "Oh!" Jenny said in dismay. The house, the lovely farmhouse she'd always imagined, stared at them like the wounded survivor of a long war.

Not one window remained intact, the porch leaned tipsily toward the ground, the splendid pillars were gone, the front door sagged drunkenly on one hinge, and the house was surrounded by litter and debris.

Grandpa drew his hand across his eyes. "Well," he said. "Well." His voice was harsh. Jenny tried to take his arm, but he freed himself. He stood in the gaping doorway, the key he had brought useless in his hand. "Let's go in."

The front room should have had ivy-printed wallpaper, massive pieces of dignified furniture, crisp white curtains, and a glass-fronted cabinet where Grandpa's grandma had kept her "gizmos," little objects of beauty that she admired—seashells, a fan, a painted cup, a glazed flowered vase.

In bewilderment and growing pain Jenny looked around. The room was stripped, bare, destroyed. The floor was ankle-deep in debris, moldering leaves, beer bottles, broken glass, unidentified filth, and grease-stained papers. What remained of the wallpaper hung in long, ugly yellowish strips, and on the bare plaster walls messages were scrawled—"Sybil and Martin" . . . "Gertie, meet me here" . . . "If anyone calls, tell 'em I'm dead" . . . "Tea for two, baby" . . . And in between the messages, obscene words appeared time and again.

Jenny's chest began to ache. She was afraid. It was so awful. She saw rocklike animal droppings in the corners. "Let's try another room, Grandpa."

He didn't move. "This was the parlor," he said. "It was the best room with all my grandmother's best furniture. It was still here, right up to the time those people were renting ten years ago." He put out his hands as if seeking support.

"Listen, maybe this is the worst," Jenny said. "Maybe it's not all this bad." She pulled open a door that protested raspingly, and picked her way through more filth. It was mostly the same thing, except that in this room there was a squat coal- and wood-burning stove. It was rusty, the door hung open, and the little windows that should have been covered with isinglass were empty. But the chimney pipe was still intact.

"Grandpa, this room isn't so bad," Jenny called. "We'll clean it up and everything will look a whole lot better. And we have a stove. Come on in, Grandpa."

Jenny found a stub of a broom in a corner and began sweeping vigorously, pushing the debris into piles, gathering up armfuls, and dumping everything through the empty window to the ground outside. Fairly soon she was filthy, but the floor was cleared, if not clean, and the whole room looked better.

Inside a closet she found a narrow dark staircase that led to the upstairs. Here there was more dirt and ruin; at her approach a bat, squeaking, flew up into a hole in the ceiling. Exploring, Jenny found a rocking chair with a missing rocker, several wooden boxes, and a metal bed frame with wire springs. She dragged all these useful things to the head of the stairs, and then one at a time brought them down.

She set the bed near the window in the clean room ("their room," as she already thought of it) and made Grandpa sit down on the broken rocker.

"Imagine when we get a fire going in the stove," she said. "It'll really be cozy." She kept her voice strong and cheerful. Grandpa, shocked by the condition of the house, had hardly moved for the past few hours. "It's going to be nice," she said. "It's really going to be wonderful, Grandpa." If she closed her eyes to slits, it seemed as if she could already see them sitting in front of a glowing fire, talking and eating, safe and snug in their own house.

# Chapter 24

"Grandpa, where do we get water?" Jenny's hands and arms were filthy from the clean-up work, and her throat felt parched. The old man, who had been sitting in the lopsided rocker, pointed to the dark, cave-like room that had been, he said, a washing-up room. "It's spooky," Jenny said. There were shelves on the walls, covered with layers of dirt and seeds, and a water pump on a rotting platform.

"Cistern is in the cellar," Grandpa said, following her in. "It gives fresh rainwater the year round." Jenny pumped the handle vigorously up and down until her arm arched, but the only result was a rusty protest from the mechanism.

"Might be the leathers are dried out," Grandpa said. "Or might be the cistern is empty." He opened the cellar door, opposite the washing-up room. "Careful, Grandpa!" Instead of stairs, there was a gaping hole opening into a dank, musty darkness. The stairs were gone. One more step and he would have plunged straight down.

"That's weird," Jenny said, holding Grandpa's arm. "No steps. How did people get down there? Where are the steps?"

"Same place the windows are," Grandpa said. "Vandals. Kids. Thieves. See something whole and they need to tear it apart. Let go of me." He stepped back, slammed the door. "Get a rock, Jenny, put it against the door. That's a dangerous place."

She found some bricks that had fallen from the

crumbling chimney, brought them in, and stacked them against the cellar door. That glimpse of stairless darkness had frightened her. If Grandpa had taken that one step and fallen—she shuddered, then told herself not to think that way. It was dangerous on Pittmann Street, too.

"We still don't have water, Grandpa," she said. She didn't mind so much being dirty, and she didn't want to upset him, but they'd need water to drink if they were going to stay on the farm.

"There's a well back of the house," he said, leading the way out the back door onto a rotting porch, the very porch where his grandmother had once sat, picking lice out of her turkeys.

All around the house, a jungle of weeds had grown up, burdock and dewberries, tall, scrawny, and vigorous, taller than Jenny and nearly impenetrable. "We could use a machete here," she said. "Ouch! They scratch."

"Scythe is what you mean," Grandpa said. Together they kicked a narrow path through the weeds to the well.

By the time they got there, they were both covered with clumps of stinging burrs that clung to their ankles and arms and tangled in Jenny's long hair. The well, too, was overgrown, and Jenny tore away the weeds to get to the rotting wood cover. The well, flush with the ground, was stone-lined. A cool wave of air rose to fan her face and, looking down into the well, she saw her own wavering reflection and the sky behind her.

Nearby, Grandpa found a metal pail half choked with dirt and lashed with a leather harness. He knocked out the dirt and then, groaning as he knelt, lowered the pail into the well. Jenny knelt on the ground next to him, watching as it tipped into the water. Hand over hand on the leather harness, Grandpa drew it up. "Heavy," he grunted, setting the pail on the ground.

Jenny plunged her hands into the clear, cold water and drank from her cupped palms. Grandpa drank for a long time from the lip of the pail, his Adam's apple bobbing in his skinny neck; then he swished water inside his mouth and spit it out. "This is the water God made," he said. "Pure water, not filled with chemicals."

At noon they sat down to eat their lunch under an apple tree in the field next to the house. The tree was old and had thick knobby branches spread wide and low, heavy with apples. The ground, too, was covered with fruit, some of it bruised, some wormy, but most of it strong, fleshy fruit that Jenny bit into with pleasure. She leaned back against the trunk of the tree. Below, the valley was filled with a pure bright light, and the sun was warm on her legs.

"In the spring," Grandpa said, "I'll make a garden. Not too big. Have to fence it against the rabbits and 'chucks. I'll plant squash, carrots, cabbage, potatoes . . ." His hands worked as he spoke, laying out the neat rows, carefully setting in the seed, and pulling weeds. "Eh," he said on a long sigh, "this is the place. The place for a man to come. It's been waiting for me. It's hurt and ruined, but it's quiet and peaceful." He nodded. "Things can be fixed and patched, and when I'm tired of working, I'll come out here and rest and look off down there into the valley and think of things and remember things."

Jenny closed her eyes. With Grandpa's spirits restored, she felt happy and contented. She didn't feel like thinking too far ahead. She dozed off easily into a bright swarming dream of animals and running and great patches of sunlight.

Later in the afternoon she found several sheets of corrugated tin that had blown off the barn roof. She dragged the straightest sheet back to the house to show Grandpa. "Useful," he agreed. "We can cover a window with it."

Jenny rummaged in the barn on a splintery shelf

and found a box of rusted nails, but no hammer. "Never mind," Grandpa said, and he showed her how to use a potato-sized stone to bang the nails into the sheet of tin, which he held in place over the empty window of their room.

Some time after, Jenny went to the outhouse, but walked out almost immediately. "Grandpa," she called. The old man was picking jagged shards of glass off the ground and throwing them into an empty five-gallon oil can. "Grandpa, I have to go, but I don't think I can use the outhouse."

He straightened up slowly, one hand to his chest. "Now, listen here, Jenny, this isn't the city. No flush toilets. Now I'm sorry, but—"

She shook her head. "I don't mean that. I don't mind using it, but I don't think it's any good anymore. I mean, there's no hole under the seat, just dirt right up to the seat."

"Well, let's go see," he said.

She was right. The outhouse, a tiny tarpapered shack leaning with the wind, had a rough wooden three-seater, but it was useless because earth had mounded up flush to the seats.

"I don't understand it," Grandpa said.

"It's not—you know," Jenny said, looking in. "It's just dirt. We could shovel it out."

"A five-foot hole, that's what's needed for an outhouse." Grandpa looked at his hands. "Five-foot hole-digging is young man's work."

"*I* could," Jenny said, "if I had a shovel. I'd do it."

Grandpa started back toward the house, then, remembering Jenny's problem, he turned and said, "Go out there in the fields, Jenny, and make yourself a cat hole. Do your business, then cover it good."

Jenny pushed her way through the weeds into a field, looking around for a sheltered place. She chose a spot under a small twisted sumac, and with a stick dug a shallow hole for herself.

A breeze fanned her hot face. Well, Jenny, she told

herself, this is how the pioneers did it.

The sun went down abruptly at the end of the day, and as it sank, cold and darkness descended. Grandpa built a fire in the stove with paper and twigs, and Jenny fed it bits and pieces of wood she'd picked up throughout the house. "Lucky the chimney wasn't busted like everything else," Grandpa said. He sat on the broken rocker, head back, eyes closed in weariness. "Ought to go look and see if that chimney is drawing okay."

"I will," Jenny said, jumping up.

Outside, she stood away from the house, neck craned, watching the smoke puffing up from the chimney. The fire gave a soft inner glow to the old house and night smoothed out the destruction it had suffered. The smoke, catching in the branches of the trees, drifted downward to the ground. There were dark clouds massed on the horizon. Jenny wondered if it would rain that night. Her family seemed very far away.

Inside she pulled a wooden box in front of the stove and she and Grandpa shared apples from the apple tree and the rest of the cheese and crackers. A soaking weariness filled her. She had been moving since dawn, not eaten much, only cat-napped, and had worked hard all day. Her hands were swollen and scratched from the banging, digging, and dragging she'd been doing all day. She bent forward, her head on her knees. With the tin up over the windows and the fire glowing in the stove, the room was really cozy. Her eyes closed, opened, then closed again.

"Jenny." Grandpa's hand was on her shoulder. "Bedtime." They lay down on the bare bedsprings, covered with Grandpa's coat and her jacket. Smoke puffed from the stove. "Need isinglass in that," Grandpa said.

There was an intense hush, and then a gradual upsurge of strange small noises, scamperings behind the walls, chittering and rustling sounds overhead. In another part of the house, a shutter banged, and trees creaked against the roof. The wind blew up higher, rattling the tin. A chill shook Jenny and she huddled closer to Grandpa, wishing she had a blanket, aware of the bare springs pressed into her sides. Nevertheless, she slept. Nothing could have kept her awake.

Much later, she half sat up, feeling stiff and cold. Something had awakened her. There was a flickering light in the room, casting long strange shadows over the wall. Grandpa was standing by the bed. "Grandpa," Jenny said. In the dim light of the dying fire she saw his face, sagging and bewildered. As if he had no idea where he was or why he was there.

"Grandpa," she said again. He didn't answer. Something caught in her throat. "Grandpa—" She reached out, touched him, groped, found his hand. "I'm here, Grandpa," she said, "I'm here."

She didn't know if it was that, or the touch of her hand, but he lay down next to her, sighing deeply. She put her arms around him, and that way they fell asleep again.

## Chapter 25

Jenny woke with the dawn. The house was dark and still. Outside, filling the air, birds were calling. Far off, cows called impatiently. Grandpa was gone.

Jenny pushed aside his coat and got out of bed. She looked around the room, seeing the dirt and ruin afresh in the clear morning light. "Grandpa," she called, "Grandpa, where are you?"

She ran to the door, suddenly afraid. The ground was wet and she saw his trail through the silvered grass. He was gathering wood, bending slowly to pick up the blowdown under the maples. A shiver shook her. "Grandpa, your coat," she called. "You ought to have your coat. It's chilly." She brought the coat to him and kissed him good morning on his rough, unshaven cheek.

She washed her hands and face in icy well water, then followed her path through the fields for her morning "business." For breakfast they ate a plate of apples. The fruit was mealy, but sweet, and Jenny, famished, ate half a dozen. It was only when she was on her sixth apple that it occurred to her there might be worms in them. She turned the apple slowly. Nothing. Thank goodness! But just then in the apple Grandpa was eating, she saw a small green worm.

"Grandpa! A worm. Stop eating. Wait—" she cried.

He continued chewing. "Only meat, Jenny," he said and calmly swallowed.

"Oh, Grandpa!" She hugged him, laughing, and covered his bristly face with kisses.

\* \* \*

Their diet all day was apples and well water. Jenny's stomach rumbled, and she decided that if she had to eat another apple she would scream. But she ate a dozen more apples and she didn't scream. Anything was better than being hungry.

In New Sayre they could buy food and other things they badly needed, but New Sayre was eight miles away and had telephones and buses. What if Grandpa insisted she get on one of those buses and go home?

"Grandpa, if my parents agree to let me live with you, will you agree?" she said.

He put down the wood he'd been stacking near the stove. "They won't agree. Look around you, child. Do you think they'd let you live here?"

"We won't let them see it this way," she said. "We'll do things, we'll make it look terrific. We'll fix it up." Closing her eyes, she imagined how the room would look when they were done.

First of all, glass in the window, not that ugly rusted tin! Then a pretty flowered curtain hanging there to draw at night and two cots with blankets neatly folded at the foot. Shelves on the wall for pots and pans, dishes, and glasses. More shelves for cans of tuna fish, tomato soup, peas, and pineapple juice. And a row of silver canisters, each one filled to the brim with important food like raisins, flour, sugar, cocoa, tea, and oatmeal. They'd have a wooden table with two wooden chairs, and candles and kerosene lamps for light. Hooks on the wall for clothing, and a big enamel basin for washing.

Later that day, while poking about in the barn, Grandpa found two old burlap feed bags printed with "White's Feed & Grain Store" in a semicircle. He brought the bags to their room, saying they could use them as covers at night. Jenny shook one vigorously and dust flew. She sneezed and took the bag outside to shake and beat against the side of the house.

"If we find some more," Grandpa said, "we could

stuff them with straw and use them for a mattress."

Jenny was off at once to the barn to search. Grandpa followed her, moving slowly. In the dimness of the barn, Jenny darted from one recess to another while Grandpa groped about under the old milk cans, bales of barbed wire, and tangles of leather harnesses. Eventually they found four more burlap sacks and set to work filling them. It was dusty, scratchy work, and Grandpa coughed continually.

In their room Jenny laid the filled bags crosswise on the springs and then flopped down to try them out. "Ooof!" Straw pricked her. Dust tickled her nose. She sneezed. The bags didn't quite reach the bottom of the bed, and her feet dragged down. But at least it wasn't bare springs.

In front of the fire that night, as they once again ate apples, Jenny made mental lists of some of the things they must have: blankets, cots, window glass, shovel, hammer, rake, scythe, lime for the outhouse pit that would have to be dug, soap, basins, towels, buckets . . .

She yawned loudly again and again, her eyes gritty. She'd planned to go outside and look at the stars, but instead staggered to the bed and collapsed on the hay-filled burlap bags. "Ouch, they're stiff," she said, and that was the last thing she remembered until the morning.

At noon the next day Grandpa lay down on the grass under the apple tree to rest. He had been moving more and more slowly, saying less and less. The sun was high and pale behind the clouds; the fields full of faded purple asters and limp goldenrod were motionless.

Jenny went to the well for water, drawing the bucket up with both hands, the water sloshing over the side. A chill breeze sprang up, and she shivered, thinking of winter. Would they draw up water the same way?

With both hands on the metal handle, she carried

the bucket to their room and set it down. She looked around, dissatisfied. As hard as she'd worked, the room was still nothing. Drab and depressing. Poverty! Her parents would hate it. Her stomach rumbled and grumbled loudly. She was dirty. She was hungry. She sat down on the feed sack mattress, irritated and tearful. What were they going to do? They couldn't live in this awful place! They'd never make it.

She sat that way for a while, then jumped up. No wonder Grandpa wasn't so sure of keeping her, if she was going to act like this! She grabbed the broom stub and began sweeping and singing loudly, "Kook-a-berra sat in the old gum tree-ee, merry merry king of the bushes, he-ee! Laugh, kook-a-berra, laugh, kook-a-berra, gay your life must BE!"

The singing cheered her and she went to stand in the door and look out over the fields. There was a noonday hush in the world. Grandpa was still asleep under the apple tree. She stood there, listening to the buzz of insects, watching him. He was motionless—as still and silent as the fields. Grandpa? She formed the word silently, then ran toward him.

In his sleep he chewed his lips. "Grandpa," she said quietly, overcome with relief. His eyelids, thick and pale, fluttered, then opened. He looked at her blankly. "Do you want a drink of water?" she said. After a moment he nodded, and groaning, he got up from the ground.

Later in the day, thick purple clouds brought a stiff, cold breeze blowing through the windowless house, rattling the tin and making the trees creak. Grandpa had sat inside most of the afternoon in front of the fire, coughing and saying little. His mouth worked silently as if he were framing thoughts.

That night the room was cold and damp, and under the sacks and their coats Jenny huddled close to Grandpa. He coughed continually, and his breath, wheezing in and out of his chest, sounded thin and frail. He needs hot soup, Jenny thought sleepily. I'll hitch into New Sayre tomorrow for sure, buy food, aspirin, cough medicine. Supermarket first. I'll buy dried soups—easier to carry—sugar, cereal, some other stuff. Her eyelids dropped down like lead. She tried to keep planning, but everything became jumbled. She heard Grandpa coughing and coughing, and then she sank into sleep.

The storm woke her. Lightning split the sky in long jagged streaks and thunder burst overhead, shaking the house. A war was going on in the sky! The trees hissed and bent in the wind. Water blew in around the sheet of tin covering the window and spattered them. Jenny pulled a sack over her head. Water began to leak from the ceiling. Her legs were getting wet. "Grandpa, you wet?" she said at last. "I'm getting soaked."

They got up and, in the dark, pushed the bed away from the window. Grandpa hacked and spit. Jenny felt as bedraggled and irritated as a wet cat. She fell onto the bed, pulled a sack over herself, shivered and shook, but fell asleep again almost at once. She never heard the storm end. When she woke the next time, all was still and silent, except for the soft patter of rain dripping from the leaves of the trees. She had been dreaming that Grandpa kissed her and said, "It's not useful, Jenny." Or perhaps it was, "No use, Jenny." Something of that sort.

A long finger of icy moonlight shone around the window tin. Cold and sleepy, Jenny moved closer to Grandpa. His side of the bed was empty. "Where are you, Grandpa?" she said. Her breath puffed frostily into the air. It was cold, very cold, the coldest night yet. Shivering, she curled tighter under the feed sacks. "Grandpa?" Already she was heavy with sleep, her eyes closing. She thought that in a few moments she would wake again and make sure he had come back to bed.

# Chapter 26

The chill morning air lay clammily in the room. The fire had gone out, and the floor near the window was wet. Grandpa wasn't in bed. She pulled on her sneakers and jacket and, hugging her arms around herself, went to the door.

There was a thin coating of frost on the ground. Every blade of grass was stiff with silver frost, and there was a deep hush over the land. "Grandpa, hello," she called shivering. "Good morning. I'm up. Where are you?" Dancing on the cold ground, she looked around for him. The silence struck her as very strange, until she realized that the wind had died down completely. Nothing was stirring.

She was hungry and started for the apple tree. Halfway there she saw Grandpa lying under the tree. Sleeping? She stopped, puzzled. On the cold wet ground? She ran the rest of the way, the stiff frozen grass swatting her ankles.

Grandpa was lying on his side, one hand up to his face. His feet were bare, white and frail looking, with thick horny nails. His mouth was slightly open, his eyes closed. He looked as he had the noon he lay down to nap in the sun.

Grandpa? she said in her mind. Are you sleeping? But she knew at once that he wasn't. It was something else, something terrible and final that at first she didn't want to name. She bent over him, and touched his face. A hand was squeezing her, squeezing her, squeezing the breath out of her. She took his arm, shook it harder and harder. "Grandpa. Grandpa, please. Please, Grandpa!"

She flung herself against him. "Don't," she cried. "Don't do this!" His body resisted hers, as if pushing her away. She sat up, looking around as if there might be someone who could help her. A red-wing blackbird lighted on one of the stiff, tall grasses and whistled.

"He's dead," she said. The words sounded stupid and senseless. At once she put her head down on his chest and listened. Had he been out here ever since she woke after the storm and found him gone?

For a long time she sat next to him on the wet ground, brushing away the flies that tried to settle on his lips. The sun moved higher in the sky, pale and partially obscured by clouds. She smoothed his hair, stroked his hands and, bending over him, put her cheek against his.

Once she began to dig a hole, scrabbling out the earth with her fingers. She wanted to bury him, right here under the apple trees. Sweat ran down her back, her arms ached, and she had to stop and rest. On her knees she dug again, with a stick and then a stone to scoop away the earth. She was able to make only a shallow hole, not long enough, not deep enough. Without a shovel she could never hope to dig a grave. She gave it up. Flies buzzed around Grandpa's mouth and eyes. She pulled grass, made a grass whisk, and kept them away. She hated their greeny-black bodies, red eyes, and ugly, hairy feet.

The sun passed to the other side of the house. Jenny went to the wet fields and picked asters and goldenrod, fading purple, fading gold, royal colors, an overflowing armful, more and more until they spilled out of her arms. She carried the flowers to the apple tree and put them on Grandpa. But it seemed silly to see Grandpa with flowers covering his chest and his chin. Impatiently she brushed them off and laid them all around him.

It was getting late. The day was passing. Jenny felt stiff and chilled, hungry and thirsty. She ate an apple, went to the well for water, and while there thought to wash her hands and face.

She went back to Grandpa and it seemed important to arrange the flowers again. She didn't want to leave him. She hadn't ever wanted to leave him. She brushed flies off his mouth. "Goodbye, Grandpa," she said. Then she set out down Turkey Hill Road, down the two hills, to the main road to find a house and people.

*Chapter 27*

The day that Grandpa died, when Jenny ran down the road, when she ran two miles to the nearest house and, knocking on the door, begging for help—that day, her mother, hearing Jenny's voice on the phone for the first time in nearly a week, having worried and suffered over her, hardly reproached Jenny at all.

"Come home," she said. "We want you to come home." And when her mother heard that Grandpa was dead, she said, "We never thought of the farm, we just didn't think of it. Oh, if we had only thought of it in time, we might have saved him."

Jenny went home on the bus. Grandpa's body was collected by the State Police. Due to the circumstances under which he died, an autopsy was required. The autopsy report showed that Carl George Pennoyer, white, male, aged eighty-three, had had an undetected case of cancer of the throat, and had been suffering from bronchitis, but that death had come as a result of exposure.

The funeral was held quietly. The family was exceptionally nice to Jenny in the days that followed. "You must have been scared," Gail said respectfully, and Valerie told Jenny about death rituals in different societies. Her parents put up with her silences and brooding moments. They didn't ask her to do anything in the house and allowed her to stay out of school several more days.

Nobody mentioned Grandpa within Jenny's hearing. If she tried to say anything about him, they changed the subject. About their running away to the farm and about his going out in the night to the apple tree, Gail blurted out that Grandpa had been crazy. She was hushed at once, but Jenny understood that this was what they all felt. They didn't want her to think about any of it. They didn't want her to brood, be morbid, or unhappy. "It's a blessing to forget," her mother told her.

Jenny, however, thought about Grandpa every day. She didn't forget him, or anything that had happened. She thought about why and how he had died, and worked it all out in her mind.

Barefoot, coatless, he had gone out into the velvety night, in the aftermath of the storm, followed the wet path to the old tree and lain down under the dripping branches. He hadn't been out of his mind, crazy, or senile. He hadn't fallen and been unable to rise. He had known exactly what he was doing, she was sure of that.

Neither of them had said it to the other, but they had both known they couldn't make it at the farm. Living there had been a fine, beautiful, and impossible dream. There had been too much decay and destruction, and Grandpa had not had the strength left to cope with years of ruin. But rather than go back and let himself be put into a home, to sit all day in a numbered chair and look at pictures blinking across a TV screen, he had gone outside and gone to sleep. No, she mustn't say that. He had died. He had hated it when people didn't say what they meant, covering up a true word with a phony one. She seemed to hear him say in his harsh voice, *I haven't gone to my final rest. I'm dead.*

She began school again, and walked every morning with Rhoda. After school, she played with Ethel, did homework, and helped her mother. On Saturdays she went to the movies, shared caramel corn with Rhoda, and shopped for shoes or a new skirt. After a while she was able to laugh at Ethel and elephant jokes, and everyone seemed pleased and relieved because she was being normal again.

"She's gotten over it already," she heard her mother say to her father. "The young have short memories."

"It's a blessing," her father said.

Unobtrusively one day the Boston rocker disappeared, along with the few other things that had remained to Grandpa. Later, a new color TV set came in, and there was talk of buying wall-to-wall carpeting for the living room. Gail began to complain about Jenny, and Frankie was deprived of his allowance for a month for failing math. Life was normal again.

One Friday night, Mr. and Mrs. Duvail, friends of Jenny's parents, came to the house to play cards. The green card table was set up in the living room. Mrs. Pennoyer brought out coffee with the best cups and a Danish pastry with thin, sweet white frosting. Valerie came upstairs to be introduced to the company; Frankie left the house to run, and Gail went to a party. As Jenny sat at the dining room table doing her homework, she couldn't help overhearing the conversation in the next room.

". . . a tough old bird," her father was saying. "He was the type who wanted to die with his boots on. And he did, God bless him."

"Frank means he was never really bedridden."

"Wonderful thing."

The voices murmured. They were sad and satisfied. "He was really a clean old man."

"That's just what I was saying to Gerald."

"Toward the end," Mrs. Pennoyer said, "he was a little confused, but what could you expect? Eighty-three."

"A good long life," Mr. Pennoyer said. "I won't kick if I live that long."

"Eighty-three! A wonderful age." That was Mrs. Duvail.

"They don't make them like Pop anymore. Here,

have some more cake, Gerry. Amelia baked it specially for you."

Jenny put her head down on the table, her arms over her ears, but she could still hear them, going on and on about Grandpa: ". . . he just lay down and died, as if he knew it was his time . . . didn't suffer a bit . . . a real comfort to us that he went so easily . . ."

Who are they talking about, she wondered. Who? And then she had to get out of there. She had to run out of the house, run and run, run as if she'd never stop, run long enough to outrun the sad, hypocritical voices. Run until the voices were gone and she could again remember Grandpa the way he really had been, and the way he always would be to her—just Grandpa.